Trojan Moon

George Woodward

authorHOUSE™

1663 LIBERTY DRIVE, SUITE 200
BLOOMINGTON, INDIANA 47403
(800) 839-8640
WWW.AUTHORHOUSE.COM

First published by AuthorHouse 08/26/05

ISBN: 1-4208-6653-2 (sc)

Library of Congress Control Number: 2005905520

Printed in the United States of America
Bloomington, Indiana

This book is printed on acid-free paper.

To my wife Jeanette
and
kids Catherine, Adam, Daniel

TABLE OF CONTENTS

PRELUDE

EARTHDATE	:	2075
DESTINATION	:	LUNAR BASE DELTA
NAME	:	MIKE BRETT
DESIGNATION	:	SPACE ENGINEER FIRST CLASS

As he handed over his plastic travel documents the announcements floated around the departure hall in multi-coloured hues corresponding to the audio signals emitted by flight control. As each announcement came and went those affected seemed to check their wrist communicators in synchronised actions, prompted by the vibro-probes, momentarily taking their attention away from the game featured on the giant hologram screen floating above their heads. The Global Series was in its final Quarter. As usual it was Europa Majors versus America Eagles. As usual the America Eagles were taking the result down to the wire and giving the fans a thrilling knife-edge finish.

Reluctant aficionados signed off and made their way to Central Dispersal Dome. Here they would be elevated to the inner section where their designated magnodiscs were waiting to spiral them across the kilometre wide departure gate carousel. The carousel moved in a clockwise direction, unusual in that most other ports preferred anti-clockwise rotation, but then the Anglos were inclined to eccentricity like that. Mike checked his own wrist communicator again and then settled down whilst the disc did its job. It finally deposited him at Space Portal 23 where the Corporate Check In Supervisor correctly acknowledged his title and status and steered him through to the VIP lounge.

As he looked back through the gate, his thoughts took him back to happier times, when he and Jasmine would take their annual vacations in Northern Europe, destination Switzerland. Here they would meet up with many friends doing the same, loosely called the "Inn Crowd". They would lose their friends and spend their time together, gliding across the permanently frozen Lac Lucerne on primitive strap-on ice skates, dancing their nights away to the strains of classical music. Even though there were many couples on the ice, they only ever had eyes for each other. Having danced their fill through to morning, they would return to their chalet, cheeks red and glowing from the cold. They would complete their evening as they made endless love on the authentic sheepskin rug spread in front of a blazing log fire. How he longed to see her now, running for the gate before it closed in preparation for boarding. Sadly not to be this time.

"Nice to see you back Sir!"

A vaguely familiar voice shattered his reverie as he focused on the young man standing before him.

"Hello Jack. Congratulations on your graduation and assignment. I could tell you would be one of the first apprentices to make it. Are you Lunar base designate?"

"Yes Sir I am."

"Call me Mike, please! The formalities are over now

Jack. School is finally out remember?"

"OK thanks Mike. What's it like up there? I mean I've studied all the vid tapes and picture libraries of course, but you're the only person I know who's actually been and worked up there. Does the simulation really do it justice? Is it really tranquil and peaceful on the surface? Do we ever get the chance to actually walk on the surface?"

Mike sighed tolerantly inside. All the new grads went through pretty much the same routine. Eager to get to the "romantic" Moon to join the growing numbers of would-be settlers, all the new recruits acted like over-excited schoolboys on the first day of term. He had done exactly the same when he first went up and knew the feeling of excitement well. In truth he still got a huge kick at the prospect of another tour of duty up there.

"It's everything you've ever heard Jack and probably more. Just remember that once the Corporate Tour ends, the hard work begins immediately. You have a three-month trial tour before your final assessment. Then, if you cut it, you're given either a permanent assignment or you're summarily shipped back Earthside for re-assessment and re-assignment, it's as simple and harsh as that. My advice my friend, enjoy it whichever way it goes. It's an unforgettable experience that much is for sure!"

Jack chattered away excitedly for another 20 minutes or so, and Mike indulged his young friend. He liked Jack, even though he still held a few reservations about his stability. He was a good engineer beyond any doubt, and they needed those with a vengeance these days. It was just a feeling he had about Jack's temperament under stress and duress. When the unexpected happened on Lunar base, it was usually not for the best and needed cool heads and dependable skills to avoid disaster. There was nothing but a gut feel where Jack was concerned, nevertheless it was there and it bothered him.

He tuned Jack out and his thoughts strayed back to Jasmine. He held back the inevitable wave of frustration that threatened to overwhelm him whenever he thought of her. He was angry with himself for being so stupid as to let her go like that. He had only himself to blame. He had taken time out on his leave time, his first time without her, to reflect on his foolishness. Their plans with each other had been so solid, so tangible, and so invincible. He had thought nothing could break them. How ironic then that it had been he himself who had destroyed their dream. Sorrow, however deeply felt, was no excuse for his behaviour towards her. Face it, he'd been an ass! He'd give anything to have the chance to convince her of that. That opportunity seemed quite unlikely now. She had made a point of getting as far away from him as she could at the time, up there on the Moon, their silly romantic lover's Moon. That was one of the reasons he had battled to tender and win the contract for the job. His company was one of the best Space Engineering Companies around. Even so he had beaten off some stiff competition and seriously under quoted on the job just to be there, on the off chance that he might find her and work things out somehow.

"Tell you what Jack," he forced himself back to reality, "why don't I have you assigned to work alongside my ground crew at Lunar Base? That way I can keep a friendly eye on your progress and throw any tasty assignments I can your way for the theoretical. What do you say?"

"You'd really do that for me? Wow! Thanks Mike, that's a real bonus! Thanks!"

Thankfully the chattering ceased as they were ushered

to their seats for take off. Mike was escorted to First Class as befitted his rank and seniority as Chief Engineer. As usual he had opted for an isobooth, giving him privacy and solitude on the 20-hour trip. He was asleep before the attendants had completed pre-flight briefing.

Jasmine felt put out again! This was the fourth joint conference she had been excluded from. She was determined to get to the bottom of what seemed to her an all too regular and irritating event. She would have words with Rick! She didn't want any favours. It was after all her responsibility as Operations Director to be up to speed on all the developments on the project. Dammit that was her job! She knew of course who was behind the omission ----- Paul ------- who else! He was acting more like a guard dog these days rather than Rick's Aide de Camp. He might well be the Security Officer and Rick's right hand man, but if he thought he could outmanoeuvre her again he needed to be firmly put back in his cage! This time he had been really too smart for his own good. A last minute meeting and she hadn't been included in signals, and only he issued the signals. Too bad! The meeting was already underway, and, following their strict protocols was sealed in behind locked doors until it was over. Sitting down at the nearest terminal she entered her user name and logged on. She quickly scanned the duty rosters. Good! She saw an opportunity to make herself scarce. If they needed her input for their precious calculations, then they'd have to come and get her. Only she had the priceless coded sequencer. She checked out her shuttle and left the base.

It was time. If he entered the symbols now whilst they slept or enjoyed their off time, there was very little chance of detection. He cursed his lack of knowledge of the finer operations of the complex. Like so many others, he had rapidly lost interest in it once their attention was focused on Exodus. His instincts had been totally correct. The Event had been and gone, and his preparations had been more than adequate. Now the time would come when he could finally lay claim to his rightful position. It was not his fault that his birthline had been disgraced, dishonoured and stripped of all power. He had been actively pursuing his commercial interests on Terrania when the Grand Council had denounced and humiliated his family, and by association he along with them. Only because he alone had the foresight to cover all eventualities would he be in any position to reclaim what was his. They would soon discover that their plans had been thwarted and that the new "Masters" would learn the meaning of real power soon enough. He had time!

He fingered the console before him. A multitude of symbols and colours filled the screen. "Akran te Sant ur!" At this command, the screen dissolved to one filled with binary sequences. Satisfied that the command was securely locked into place, Lloran closed down the computer, exited the room and locked and sealed the outer hatch.

"Mr President Sir!" The presidential Aide was rewarded after the third buzzer.

"Yes! What is it?"

"Operation Trojan Sir. We just got the signal two minutes ago. Message reads ' Helen in the City. STOP. Gift of the Gods at the Gate'."

"Very well. Thank you. Goodnight."

"Goodnight Sir."

CHAPTER ONE: TRAGEDY

Mike stared in disbelief. The flickering screen before him could not be right. A tremor of that size on the scale indicator was just not possible. Not there!

Quickly recalibrating the complex settings, he had barely activated the reset tab, when the screen threw another "wobbler".

"What the hell......!" Mike exclaimed. "Who's messing with the mainframe?" he shouted. The Quorum team turned as one to look at him, six identical frowning faces seeking further data.

Although it seemed like he had grown up with it, Mike could still not get used to the application of these new developments in human resource management and the duplicating processes recently perfected. Even though the discovery had almost overnight revolutionised the manning of the satellite research teams, which seemed to dominate all research projects these days, he still shivered inwardly in their presence.

"Never mind, never mind," he muttered irritably to himself, "back to stations!"

The background noise of tweeting consoles and clicking buttons resumed as the almost translucent work team obeyed simultaneously. "Great help you lot are!" He muttered to himself again in bad humour and returned his attentions to the monitor.

Before he had the chance to examine the printout pouring from the console, Earth Control chimed through on the communications channel. The normally friendly face of David Colton filled the screen with a countenance of undisguised anger.

"Mike! Are you fooling around up there?" he barked

"No way Sir" he replied.

"Then what in Trills name happened to the monitors?" came the insistent, almost impatient and, to Mike's mind, panicky barrage of questions

"I'm working on it right now David, what do you see down there? That last impulse jumped off the scale."

"Exactly the same as you, obviously," said David, visibly calmer now.

"Just a moment Mike" said David as the sound of an Earth Control communications alarm sounded.

He waited patiently, then noticed yet another change in David's face again. Concern and irritation gave way to incredulity swiftly followed by a fleeting glimpse of horror before he turned back to face Mike's monitor.

"We just lost Lunar One." he said almost robot like.

"What do you mean, lost Lunar One............,". Mike stopped mid sentence as a blurred image broadcasting from the Lunar base began to blare out an urgent appeal from the receiver to his right. "David, I've got an emergency transmission. Stand by".

"Is anyone there, anyone getting this, Oh God help us please! OK erm scary stuff,.... look OK...."

Normally the epitome of the smooth professional, Mike found it hard to equate the rambling and incoherent idiot on the screen with the normally competent and assured person he knew Jack Kidd to be. Something serious was going on for sure.

"Hell Jack what's got into you?" Mike reached for the comm. link and punched in the familiar codes.

"Jack! Jack! This is Mike Brett out on the orbit track 9631, do you copy?"

"Mike! Thank God it's you, I've been calling for 20 minutes now! Listen, do you still have communication with Lunar One?" he asked in a shaky voice.

"I... I don't know, I haven't tried them. I've been kinda busy re-setting the system. What's going on Jack?"

"Mike, it's all gone I saw buildings, vehicles, people, all floating past the tower just a few minutes ago on the monitor and..........."

"Whoa, whoa back up there a minute back up!" Mike yelled. "Take a deep breath and tell me exactly what happened. You'll be telling me next there's been an Earthquake ...."

Jack nodded frantically "So your instruments saw it too then? The quake? I thought I was going crazy! "

Jack described exactly what he'd experienced. From the coffee cup moving across the table, the low rumbling noise quickly followed by a cracking sound which built up into a roaring crescendo and then ...... sudden silence. What he described was nothing spectacular by earth standards, but here the force of the same quake was enough to have dislodged and displaced the human settlement and dome of Lunar One, almost like a dog shakes off water. The dome, buildings, plant, vehicles and personnel he imagined now travelling at a velocity of 8 clicks per second out into the blank void of space. At least 2,000 men, women and children, not to mention an investment of $60 billion had been wiped out in an instant.

3

"But hang on Jack, the Moon simply doesn't have the physics to create a quake, no tidal effects, no hot molten core. Whatever this is, it's no "Moon Quake" I'm sure of it. I'm coming in."

"Be quick Mike! I don't know if this place could withstand something that powerful a second time."

Mike thought fast. The moon station was designed to withstand any trauma known to mankind. Buried two miles under the lunar surface to avoid any danger from meteor strikes, and so self-sufficient it needed only a few people to maintain its vital functions, it housed the vast lunar working population of scientists, engineers and explorers some 5,000 in number. It was safe from any further disturbances he was sure.

Some, like him, were the corporate strategists manning the 50 or so artificial satellites circling the Moon, all conducting various research experiments.......and he was responsible for all of them he realised with a start !

"Jack, can you confirm all tubes as functioning and ready for emergency in-vac?"

"Affirmative Mike" responded Jack, regaining some of his normally dependable composure.

"Right! I'll be with you in 15 to 20 minutes. I'll try to over-fly the site, debris permitting. "

"Be careful Mike, some of those pieces are still moving at some speed and would make one hell of a mess if they connected." All efficiency and control now Jack was rebooting the console controls back to their normal functions. He felt relieved that there was someone he could hand over to, and the glimmer of hope of being rescued.

After confirming his plan to Earth Control, Mike began the preparations for the in-vac flight. In emergencies (and if ever there was an emergency this seemed like it), the satellite stations could be prepared for flight and be Moonward bound within minutes.

He closed down the running experiments, taking care to back up their findings and recordings and began the shut down routine of the Quorum team function.

The shut down of the virtual work team was the last routine to run. The spectacle still fascinated him, even after all these years. As one the six workers first seemed to waver, merged and then condensed into the containment tank. Locking the safe stow toggle, Mike returned to the pilot's seat and took manual control of the ship.

"Re-entry in 30 seconds" droned the panel voice module. Mike looked ahead at the Vid screen, noting with some unease that he was moving towards a debris-strewn sector of space. "Nothing we can't cope with," he said to himself, and settled into the padded pilot's chair.

A movement at the edge of his vision range caught his attention. Anxious to avoid any further mishaps, he focussed the Vid screen, narrowed the vector angle and magnified the image. He stared at the spinning image for a good 5 seconds before registering that it was a body .....no a pressure suit, probably flung out into space by whatever had caused the disaster displacing the dome and all its contents. Something odd caused him to hesitate before switching back to forward view. The visor in the suit was lit up! It was occupied! An emergency beacon was activated whenever the suit's wearer was in any difficulty to facilitate rescue. But surely not out here! They were at least 50 miles above the surface.

In one movement, he flicked on autopilot, exited the control seat and ran to the nearest observation window. His heart pounding, his eyes confirmed the worst. The suit was occupied and heading out into the void with no hope of return. The slowly rotating suit turned towards him and in a fleeting moment, he caught a glimpse of the occupant's face contorted with fear. He realised with horror he had only seconds to act or it would be beyond any hope of retrieval.

He yelled out the emergency halt command and braced himself as the ship was bought to a dead stop. Without breaking stride, he sprinted to the EAV, strapped himself in, and took off in the general direction of the starkly white object now looming large in the Perspex screen of the work craft. He realised he had only one chance at this.

Accelerating harshly, he put the work pod on a sharp upward drive towards the suit whilst at the same time extending the forward grabbers upward and outwards. It was a risky move. If he collided with the suit, they weighed in around one tonne each, he and his flimsy craft would be destroyed. He did not know whether the speed at which the suit was moving would overstress the manipulators as it was. All he knew was he had to try. If they were to gain any insight into the tragedy of Lunar One, he had to succeed in this. There was no way of knowing if this was the only survivor. Thinking fast, he spurred the EAV on into a faster approach, and then risking burnout to his motors, threw it into a sharp and parabolic curve to bring him onto a parallel course with the suit.

As he closed the distance, the figure in the suit saw him for the first time. He was close enough to see the face screaming at him for help and to feel the abject terror of the survivor.

"Easy now" he thought to himself as he jiggled and wrestled with the controls. The suit was travelling slightly faster than his craft's top speed. He had timed his approach too finely. In a flurry of movement, the suit shot past him and his heart sank, as he feared he had missed!

"Damn!" Then to his amazement he felt the craft lurch to one side. By chance a loose belt trailing from the suit had snagged one of the over stretched manipulators. He resisted the urge to decelerate immediately. The belt was only just checking the bulky suits flight and the last thing he wanted was to lose the grip or snap the thing completely. "Gently does it," he thought to himself and began a slow controlled reduction in speed to bring the runaway to a halt before securing his catch for the trip back to base.

The whole manoeuvre had taken less than 3 minutes but it felt more like 3 hours as he wiped away the sweat from his forehead and started back toward the ship. With satisfaction he noted that the suit appeared to be intact, although badly dented and scarred. He could see no immediate danger and decided to waste no time getting back with his catch in tow.

Once the ship was in view, Mike began to evaluate the options. He had brought off an incredibly unorthodox rescue in stopping the runaway. Now he was faced with the question of how he was going to get it on board. It certainly would not fit in the EAV bay without blocking his own return. The "cargo" door was much too small to accommodate it either. Designed to allow small tools and specimens to be taken on board the station it offered no entry point. There was only one option left open to him and he didn't like it one little bit.

He decided that his only choice was to back the EAV into its bay and "piggy-back" the suit and contents back to base outside the ship. He could just make out of the oxygen gauges located on the suit's underside showing tanks at half full. There was no way he could warn his occupant of his plans, but considering the alternative, he decided explanations later would have to suffice.

Mike reviewed his plans for base touchdown, deciding he would take the ship in manually just in case the additional load threw the auto pilot off-line.

Under way again and with the fate of his "passenger" very much in mind, Mike resumed his descent back to base, homing in on the beacon still beaming out its welcoming tone. With no further visual debris to hamper his flight, he eased the ship into the capture beam with a satisfying "clunk", and relinquished control to Moon Base Control.

Whilst waiting for the final manoeuvres, he checked his passenger was secure before returning to his seat and strapping in for docking. He radioed ahead and was relieved to find himself speaking to his usual ground crew who appeared to be working as normal at least. He quickly outlined the rescue and briefed them on the recovery procedures they should follow to retrieve their precious survivor.

"Whoever it is, I'd like to see them in the debrief room straight away" he added.

Despite the pandemonium and confusion back at base, with the excitement of the chase, rescue and return out of the way, Mike's curiosity now took hold as he hurried through the shut down routines and officially signed off his satellite mission as "aborted". Emergency procedures also appeared to be running smoothly as planned.

He exited the ship and walked the few yards to the debriefing room. To his amazement and disbelief the vision before him almost took his breath away. She was petite, blonde, beautiful… a little bruised and shaken… and as angry as hell from the look on her face.

"Are you the idiot of a pilot who brought me in?" she demanded "because if you are I'm going to * ** ** well deck you! What kind of trick do you call that? You could have killed me with that re-entry!"

"Jasmine!" exclaimed Mike "If I'd known it was you out there, I'd have waved as you sailed by on your way to Alpha Centauri!"

They both collapsed in a heap, Jasmine was laughing and crying simultaneously. She suddenly leapt up at Mike wrapping her arms and legs around him as he held her tightly whilst the tension took hold.

Jasmine almost regained her composure then seemed unable to let him go. Her relief and the overwhelming realisation of how close she had been to dying suddenly seemed to rack her body with spasms of uncontrollable shivering.

"Medics!" called Mike "delayed shock protocol NOW!"

Two medics took Jasmine gently from him, strapping her into the hypo-chamber, and rendering her unconscious, they took her swiftly to sick bay.

"Thank God!" thought Mike as he watched them go. His thoughts turned once again to the disaster at hand and what had caused it.

As Jasmine succumbed to the treatment, her mind seemed to float free as dreams of the past flooded in uncontrollably. She recalled somewhat painfully a time long ago when she and Mike were together, first as children, then as lovers and finally married. Their families were linked in friendship as well as business. Mike's father had been a prominent and gifted scientist, her father a great businessman and entrepreneur, and something of an adventurer. Together they had combined their talents to forge an alliance, which created one of the world's greatest corporations. They had created a powerful institution responsible in great part for many of the advancements and new technologies enjoyed by the people of Earth, and mostly the reason she was now here. Her involvement in the Moon project originated in the boardroom of that organisation. They were the early days when as young adults she and Mike had graduated together and being drawn into the "family" business. With their respective talents they had contributed to the progress of the corporation and it's emergence as the leading space exploration company in the world. Along the way they had found romance and true companionship in each other, without any prompting from the families, which helped in the formation of so many of the company's radical developments and progressions. Almost as if on cue at this point in the dream, as so often had happened in the past when she chose to go there, the nightmare returned. She imagined she saw staring eyes devoid of life settling into an oozing foul smelling mass of yellow coloured liquid staining the carpet at her feet. Some inner defence mechanism would flick the switch to overload and her mind descended into a black nothingness as again she slept a sleep devoid of all sensation.

CHAPTER TWO: ANALYSIS

"Here is what we know at present."

Muster of the summoned personnel had revealed depletion of the population of the base to just 2,105 personnel out of the 5,000 stationed there. Like Mike, most of the supervisory staff was on duty when the quake hit. Of the 50 control satellites his was the only craft not disabled by flying debris. By chance the vector that he had been working was shielded by the curvature of the moon. Of the other 49 stations, 40 were not responding to communications but still registered in displaced positions around the Moon. Of the other 9 there was no trace whatsoever.

Jan Keeps was the off duty Project Director at the time of the quake and it was he who now addressed the subdued and hushed briefing group.

"At 09.15 hours, all monitors leapt off the calibration scale. Lunar One was apparently sited directly above the area of seismic activity which was strong enough to rupture all seals in all the pressurised facilities and ejected the entire complex into space with the loss of over 3,000 lives that we know of so far." Grim faced Jan turned to the screen behind him.

"Our only remaining mobile satellite, Mike's, over-flew the site about an hour ago. These visuals show the view from above. Guys you may have difficulty accepting what you see as real... this is an impossibility, but I assure you it is real!"

The screen faded first to a fuzzy mass of white before gradually focussing in on the scene which showed the normal moonscape moving to begin with, then zooming in and down to a view of the site which had once been the pride of the Moon's colonists, Lunar One. Only the outline of the main dome outer ring remained as visible proof of man's activity. Everywhere there were fragments of the base now spread over miles of terrain, vehicles, furniture, clothing, and tools, anything in fact that hadn't managed to escape the gravitational pull.

The fissure was obviously deep. It seemed as though tremendous forces had torn apart the Moons crust and left a gaping chasm. Mike sensed something odd about the picture.

"Obviously the cause of the disaster" Jan elaborated for them. "This fissure has one exceptional feature." He paused and looked at them grim faced and nervously licked his lips. "It stretches from pole to pole."

A murmur of utter disbelief around the room rose to a crescendo of questions shouted out all at once. Jan's attention was drawn to his aide and beckoned him urgently. They stood together for only 10 seconds, then he called the room hastily back to order.

"Listen up everybody. All none essential personnel have been given orders for immediate emergency evacuation.

A team of investigators will stay behind to study what's happening. I want 12 volunteers."

Mike stepped forward at once and was joined by Alan, Colin, Jack and the entire West Section team leaders making up the 12.

"I want in!" came a demand rather than a request from the door to the briefing room. All heads turned. Jasmine stood there swaying slightly and holding onto the doorframe for support. "No-one is fooling around on my Moon without me!" she added, as she seemed to fold over and then collapsed on the floor.

Mike hurried over and helped her to a chair. "You shouldn't be up yet, your sedation was supposed to keep you asleep until your evacuation.........."

"Just what you would like I suppose! Sorry, sorry I'm still groggy and oh yeah I really mean a big sorry. You saved my life out there and risked your own doing it too from what I remember, and what the hospital guys were telling me." She squeezed his arm and fleetingly looked deeply into his eyes.

Any frostiness he felt before melted instantly and he felt himself compelled to return her gaze, that old familiar surge of emotion whenever he met her returned.

"Get me on the team Mike, please" she pleaded "I have got to find out if this is connected......"

" Why do you always see Machiavellian plots wherever you go?" he chided softly "Why should they would be any connection at all?"

"Just call it a hunch," she said realising her mistake too late "female intuition. Please Mike you know my speciality better than anyone. From what I've been told, I am the obvious choice for this."

She was right of course, Jasmine had qualified for the project at roughly the same time as he had but she had specialised in Lunar geology and physics, while he had opted for spacial engineering. He knew of course that her position on the Directorate of Visage Incorporated, a sub-division of the Corporation , effectively made her his boss.

"OK, I'll fix it. But only if the medics clear you first. Agreed?" He asked.

"Of course" she responded. "Now how about if I treat you to a cold drink to make peace and thank you properly." To his dubious reaction she raised an eyebrow in question stunning Mike with the sudden change in their relationship. But then again he thought to himself, close death encounters could do that to people.

"OK Jasmine, you're on. But first I have to make arrangements for these missing personnel; you know contact their families, file reports write letters and all those things expected of the section leader. You know how particular the company can be about that sort of thing and the medics will still have to give you the all clear".

Shortly after the mass evacuation of the Moon's non-essential personnel, the complex was handed over to the Earth Government agency team of coordinators and investigators who would work along side of the Visage Inc. team to facilitate the investigation into the disaster, and explore the implications of the developments on the Moon.

They got down to business with the admirable efficiency. By the end of the first day, they had put together plans for an exploratory mission to gather evidence at first hand in the hope that it would help explain the formation of the rift or the "Grand Kanyan" as it was becoming known.

Mike was to lead a team of two groups to work along the rift from the derelict camp outwards into opposite directions towards the poles where they would meet up with another section team doing the same but working inward from the poles. If any of the teams discovered anything significant they were to converge and coordinate all effort at the site. It was perhaps an optimistic and primitive approach, but given the unprecedented nature of what they were facing it seemed as good a starting point as any.

Mike, Jack, Alan, Colin and Jasmine made their final checks. Mike personally selected his faithful quorum team. He chose to use his original team above the replacement banks that had been brought in from the reserves. He felt more secure knowing the various quirks and characteristics of what was essentially his back up team if they hit trouble. They might prove an invaluable asset at virtually any stage of the expedition. He was also quite fond of Gandly, his donor worker who he had met personally on several occasions when he wasn't on secondment service. Mike was well aware that Gandly was one of the few original Quorum teams to have survived the initial 'quake and by rights he should have released him on advanced leave. Selfish as it seemed he had convinced himself to retain him for the full 6 months on-call time. Besides he hated the thought of having to break in a new duplicator team right now.

With the formalities over and the final pre-flight checks completed, Mike took the ship's controls and hit the go button. With an eager leap forward, the sturdy exploratory craft manoeuvred out of its hanger and quickly assumed its customary planet orbit. With a jolt he realised that today the well-worn path he normally followed would lead to nothing. His mind replayed the image of the bustling community of Lunar One designed to be the first stage of Man's colonisation of space.   He recalled with some sadness days spent on leave amongst his many friends there, before reigning in his feelings and setting himself the almost impossible mission of finding out what it was that had wiped out his friends. With a resolute determination, he comforted himself with the thought that death for most would have been mercifully swift.

CHAPTER THREE: GRAND KANYAN

The silence and stillness of the natural lunar landscape merely emphasised the site of utter devastation and disaster that greeted Alpha team, Mike's designated call sign. From the original station video the scene had been bad enough, but at close quarters, the full impact of the disaster that had overtaken its occupants was now only too apparent.

The rift had opened up directly down the middle of the settlement causing massive almost instantaneous depressurisation destroying the primary and secondary domes, the streets the buildings and all the contents, shaken off the surface in just a few terrifying seconds. The largest, costliest and most ambitious space project ever undertaken Lunar One had been two decades in the planning, another 8 years of organising and financing, and now after several years of the most expensive construction work, it had all been destroyed in just a few fleeting moments.

Mike allowed to ship to make touchdown well to the east of the edge of the huge gaping abyss that now stretched black and menacing as far as the eye could see. He was loath to admit it, but Mike felt a true sense of foreboding as he surveyed the moonscape outside the ship.

He secured the ship's status and made his preparations for an EVA with his normal efficiency and thoroughness. There was no room for error. With unknown factors to contemplate, he could not afford to ignore any possibility.

"Jasmine, you're with me. Allen and Colin take Number One pod and traverse the Kanyan to the other side. Jack you will be responsible for the backup quorum team, maintaining communications and the monitors. If anything does show up on the monitor yell out straightaway. Alan I want you guys to work Northwards. Check in every 25 minutes. We don't know what we're looking for exactly, but I guess we'll know it if it hits us! We'll start southwards, though I want to make a controlled descent into the abyss first to see how deep it goes. Stand by while we establish the extent of the rift before moving on. Should be some interesting discoveries along the way, who knows?" He smiled trying to give the impression he knew what was doing, and as a weak attempt at boosting morale. "OK let's do it!"

As they approached the lip of the gaping chasm, Mike slowed the pod to a steady hover. Alan had made the other side and had measured the gap at 400m, pretty much constant for as far as they could see, for about a kilometre in either direction of the landing site. Mike gave the thumbs up before proceeding with the descent into the depths.

"Beginning descent" Mike responded to Jasmine with a perfunctory "Aye!" his eyes glued to the vertical wall before them picked out by the powerful searchlight beam. 'Solid rock, cut through as if by a knife' he mused to himself. The readings themselves were nothing special, just the usual rock structure similar to the lunar surface. The sonar equipment came on-line at his command. With few landmarks by which to gauge their movement, it was all too easy to become disoriented on visuals alone. Front and rear sonar's helped keep them on-line and centred in the middle of the rift as they descended further into its depths. Other units monitored the space beneath the pod, safeguarding against the danger of bottoming out too soon.

"How far down now" asked Jasmine anxiously after 15 minutes.

"We're going in really slow" smiled Mike. "We're almost 300 m down, nothing extraordinary yet. "

They didn't speak again for 30 minutes or more, the other teams called in as routine reporting similar uneventful progress.

"Hello," said Mike, "the bottom scanner seems to be coming on-line now at 2,000 m. deep. What's the width reading Jasmine?"

"Still 400 metres" came the reply "That is so unnatural. How could a quake create such a perfectly squared section of the surface to this depth?"

Jack's voice interrupted their thoughts.

"Mike, I'm getting some readings here like I've never seen before. I can't place the source exactly, there is a steady vibration somewhere around here and it's building rapidly. Do you see or read anything unusual down there?"

"Negative." Mike responded, "Can you feed it through and let me see what you've got?"

"Will do"

"Did you see that?" asked Jasmine. "There on the east wall face. It looked like some sort of structure, metallic or something, it just reflected the beam!"

"No, didn't catch it" said Mike. "Let's take it back a little. Did you get a fix on it?" "Yep, should be on it....... now! There!"

They both stared with incredulity through the glass. To all intents and purposes it looked just like an oval flange. There was no other way to describe the shape looming up out of the gloom. Mike pivoted the craft around on its axis and directed the spotlight towards the other wall. There was a corresponding shape on that side too.

"Let's go further south at this height," said Mike. "There may well be other........"

At that moment without warning all visibility was wiped out by a blanket of dust swirling around the pod.

"Mike, get out of there double quick! I've got seismic activity all around ....rift..........unar surf......... ywhere......" Jack's transmission faded into static. Not that Mike needed any prompting. He didn't even try to restore communications. They were caught up in the swirling mass of dust clouds, which threatened to engulf the tiny craft. His prime concern was to keep the vital directional thrusters clear of debris. Without them they would be lost. Fighting against the unfamiliar turbulence, Mike struggled with the controls.

"Let's try to get nearer to the wall face. We might escape some of the bigger particles there Jaz!" Jasmine, white faced, nodded in agreement and took control of the forward thrusters whilst Mike jiggled the craft's orientation steering. Having lost their sense of direction, the pod inevitably slammed heavily into the cliff before bouncing back into the maelstrom of swirling currents that bucked and threw them around for what seemed like forever.

Seeing Jasmine was having difficulty maintaining control, Mike switched to the co-pilot's seat and helped her fight to regain control. By instinct he moved the column hard forward and was rewarded when they broke loose from the tortured atmosphere and returned back to the wall. It was then he noticed that the portal they had observed was hollow inside, with more than enough clearance for their pod. With a dexterity born of desperation, he deftly manoeuvred the pod into the structure and touched down on the lower edge to ride out the storm outside.

Now that the dust wasn't so dense they took the chance to examine their surroundings. Dull metallic in colour, the portal, was 60 m high and 40 m across. From the regularity of its lines, Mike had already fathomed that it was neither a natural, nor, logic told him, could it be a man-made structure. He was less than certain though as to its purpose and what if anything it might lead to.

"Come in Jack come in!" Jasmine was almost frenetic in her efforts to make contact. "He won't answer damn it!" she cried. "Jack! Jack! Come back you sonofabitch!"

"Jasmine! Is that you?" came a weak response. "Thank God! You're still alive! God I thought for sure you'd bought it! Listen! We've got big trouble! We're abandoning camp if we can that is,..... badly damaged......... barely airborne. I'm trying to make it back to base but the power is low and I can't seem to get off this damned crust"

"Off what? " Both Mike and Jasmine looked at each other puzzled.

"You mean you haven't seen it yet," said Jack "No of course not. Mike this is so unreal. The rate this thing is going, we have got to get off soon or we're all goners for sure. OK. I'll make this real quick. That activity I reported? It gathered pace and pitch and next thing you know, the whole surface of the Moon just lifted off! A whole segment of Moon Mike, at least a mile wide. I don't know how deep, just lifted off and floated clean away with the ship and me on board. I can see the whole thing curving as a whole piece just rising away. I'm trying to lift off, but the velocity this thing is moving at is holding us down. Mike what you suggest we do?"

'Damn you!' thought Mike as he recognised the whining panic edge crept back into Jack's voice showing how wrong the executive had been in overriding his assessment 'Can't this guy hack it under pressure?' he thought.

"Jack, get the third pod on-line, rigged for emergency escape transit! Do it now! Get moving towards the edge and switch to normal flight once you're clear! OK? You'll make it OK. Just hang on in there!"

"Right Mike" came the faint reply.

"It sounds like he's almost out of our range," said Jasmine listening through the headset. "And if he's abandoning the ship, where do we go from here? "

Mike's attention was now firmly back on their own situation. Gaping canyons, breakaway segments of Moon, impossible engineering feats below the surface of the Moon, what else was there to bother him? Ah yes, getting safely back to base! Now the dust had settled and was no longer obscuring their vision, he manoeuvred back towards the edge of the flange. He knew there was a drop of at least 1000 metres to the floor of the rift. The surface however was now only 60 metres above them! That answered one of Jack's questions at least. Looking beyond the new surface edge, he could clearly see the phenomena Jack had described. He could see not just one strip of rapidly disappearing rock above them. Mike blinked. He felt like he was seeing double! A twin strip to the one carrying Jack's ship was rising and disappearing from the other bank of the rift. "You see when I see Jaz?" he asked.

"How can that be?" she replied quietly. "What is all this Mike? Look!"

Turning back Mike could see the object of her attention. On the inner wall of the portal, pin-sized points of light flashed in a sequence of some kind.

"Patch it into the EAV computer. Let's see if it's some kind of code or message or some kind of encryption. It could even be the key to getting inside this, whatever it is" he said.

"What do we do if it is? Are you suggesting we try and get inside? We don't know what it is or what its purpose is. It could be anything. How do we know if it leads to the inside at all?"

"Let's just say our options at this moment in time are severely restricted. We can't get back to base in the EAV alone, it doesn't have the range. If Jack doesn't get off the slice of Moon he's riding, he can't come to rescue either, and if we stand and do nothing, we'll never know what we missed. I don't know about you, but I prefer action to inaction any day."

He could see the uncertainty in her eyes and relented his harsh manner.

"Look," he said softly "Jack is a good kid, he's shown he can be resourceful. If he manages to get off the debris OK, he could very well be heading back to base right now for help. If we leave the EAV here, they can home in on it and follow us through to wherever this leads. Aren't you at least curious?"

"Of course I am, and I suppose we could always leave the key if we find it for them to use."

"That's my girl" he smiled. 'Well, at least this will keep us occupied if nothing else.' he thought to himself.

In truth he knew, as did Jasmine, that their position was quite precarious. Oxygen was OK, their portable recycling units would hold out for weeks. They could carry enough fresh water for at least 4 to 5 days, with the recyclers that could extend to 10 – 15 days, assuming of course a rescue was possible, and that no other disasters got in the way.

Mike looked again at the opposite wall. Now that the surface was only a few tens of metres above them, the reflected light revealed more detail. To his amazement, the walls had the same metallic sheen as the portal. 'They must be metal too!' he realized with some trepidation 'and if they are, how far do they extend and why?' A thousand questions seemed to fill his head at once. He forced himself away from the turmoil in his head and focussed his attention on the decoder.

As the code was operating in the visible light spectrum, he arranged a scanner on a makeshift stand directing the receiver towards the light source. The sequence was flickering at great speed. Too fast for the human eye, it seemed to have a short cycle of pauses every 10 seconds or so. He set the equipment to record for 10 minutes analysis.

Back in the relative comfort of the EAV, the data was being processed.

"This might be quite a long wait. We never had the chance to talk about the moment the quake struck," said Mike. "Do you mind talking about it now?"

"No not really. Doc Grey is really good, I don't have any lingering trauma if that's what you're worried about."

"No I know you're OK, you wouldn't be on this excursion without your clearance by that Psycho" he joked. "So what did you see? How come you were the only survivor? Why were you in that suit? Care to tell me about it?"

"Hey! What is this? The third degree" she responded mocking his mood of concern just the way she used to do, accusing him with her steel grey eyes. "It's a bit boring really. I was on maintenance duty, you know, servicing the moon buggies and other operational equipment to give them their certification. I knew the instant the dome had popped because I'd been through it one time before, remember?

When the initial landing party to set the project up in the first place put up a small advance dome and flanged it up all wrong, it cracked open within minutes of being pressurized?"

" Yeah! If I remember correctly, you rescued 10 engineers."

"Sure, whatever. Anyway the effect was the same. The glass popped, the air escaping with a whoosh and then all hell broke loose. Vehicles, tools, buildings all took off and headed skyward. Same thing here, but on a much larger scale. I just happened to be working on the suit and was pulled out with the force of the depressurisation. The suit came with me and somehow, don't ask me how, I found myself inside it. I must have done it automatically, got it all sealed up and pressurized just like in the drills. Then I guess I blanked out for a while. When I came too I was being thrown around all over the place. The suit was still tethered to a mooring post. I had a simple choice – scrambled brains or cut loose. I cut loose thinking I could use the retros to steer myself out of trouble. Only thing was, it was the retros I'd been working on before the dome went. I hadn't finished refurbishing the energy packs so they were useless. So then off I sailed into the black wide yonder until some nutcase in a silver bubble came by and played snag 'n' tag with me."

"Did you see anyone else escape?" he asked.

"No. Apart from the maintenance hangar, there were no other pressure cabins anywhere around the complex. Even if there had been, they would all be in free fall now between here and the Alpha Quadrant by now."

Mike's saw her eyes moisten and quickly changed tack. He could sense there were horrors she'd seen she had rather not.

"So, what you make of this then?" he asked. "You specialised in lunar geology didn't you? Who put this here? How was it built and how come we've never registered it before now?"

"Well, look at the facts. These readings don't register the surface as anything other than rock. It may look like a metal, but it reads like rock. It has the same density and molecular structure as everything else around it."

She glanced over his shoulder. "Looks like the computer has enough data to play with."

Mike checked the recorder and brought it back inside the EAV. After about an hour of playing with the feedbacks, Michael thought there was a possible combination to look for.

"It looks like it might be an interference interlock match plate pattern.," he said eventually. "Each pulse of the light is a question, answered by a corresponding pattern in sequence until all the sequences marry up and then 'hey presto'."

"How did you figure that out?" asked Jasmine

"The company is absolute paranoid about espionage and eavesdroppers on their security codes and transmissions. I've probably studied every code possible at some point or other. As codes go, this is quite sophisticated, but not foolproof. I'm going to set the Quorum team on to the problem. Let's see if they can come up with anything."

" Won't it be a little bit crowded in here with them in action?"

"They can be adjusted you know!" Mike returned the mood of false joviality." I'll minimize them to a tenth normal size"

Once the team had been activated and briefed, he left them to it. Jasmine was dozing in the pilots seat. Mike took the co-pilot seat and settled down to await the team's results. There was no more for him to do. As he reclined fully backwards he allowed his mind to wander again.

He recalled as a young boy growing up in the leafy suburbs of Framby. Happy days watching his dad at work on his computers, fascinated by the holograms and 3D moving images all around the house. As he grew older he began working on some of his dad's projects until the old man turned to him one day and said

"Son, I've just got to show you something really special. Stay there and don't move!"

His Dad went into his study and Mike heard the usual background hum of the computers and equipment. Then came an unfamiliar sound. Almost immediately the study door opened and out came three, no six images of his dad! He watched in absolute amazement as each of them walked about the room, occupying itself with a separate activity. Mike could see that the images were translucent and in places just a little jagged. No sound came from any of them. As Mike watched, mouth agape, the images wavered and merged into one, then disappeared into a thin line of light, which exited through the study door. He followed it through the door just in time to see it enter a large metal cylindrical device standing in a corner of the room. A panel in the cylinder opened and out stepped his dad.

Beaming with pride of Tom explained to his son the principle he had established of manipulating human matter form to project itself in perfect replication many times over without losing physical ability nor agility, and without any harmful effects at all. Through the combination of harmless static electricity, and rare gases discovered on the Moon, he had created the duplicator process now known as the "Quorum" effect. Each replication of the individual was able to perform any necessary task, physical or mental, independent of the "host" or donor and independent of each of the other replicas. The only physical restriction there appeared to be was the inability to dissipate the body entirely. The one organ that could not safely be projected outside of its physical form was the eye. From experiments with animals, he had discovered quite early on that sustained exposure caused rapid deterioration of the functioning of the eye to the point of blindness within a very short time. The "host" had to be confined to a precisely controlled environment sphere with provision for the safe retention of the eyes during the period of operation. Under strict codes of security before very long, numerous banks of operating houses exploited the enormous potential of this development. Lucrative contracts were offered to potential " hosts", and there was no shortage of applicants.

Nobel Peace Prizes and worldwide recognition were to follow and once financial backing had been secured for Visage Corporation Industries, it rapidly became the key player in developing the global Colony Trail Institute, dedicated to the exploration of life beyond the boundaries of Earth. His father and his long time college buddy, Rik Strangeman, headed up this new organisation. Overnight this one successful discovery increased the pace of terrestrial study and subsequent technical advances by decades.

With the success of the corporation, sadly Mike saw less and less of his father as pressures on his expertise took him further afield to spread the good news and to share the discovery. Inevitably their close relationship drifted the way of most Father/son relationships and they spoke infrequently.

Naturally Mike followed in his father's footsteps by entering the corporation as the talented engineer he'd always been encouraged to become. All went well until that fateful night his dad called him from the Corporations prestigious Head Office in Vancouver.

"Mike, Come to my office as quick as you can! I don't have much time; I've got to move fast on this. Come now! Drop everything!"

As quick as that? No contact for weeks and suddenly a five second message summoning him? What was going on? Had he made another breakthrough discovery? That part at least was typically consistent of the man, never content to sit back and relax, always reaching for his next success. It was his nature, pursued with a passion since losing the wife, Mike's mother, he had always adored.

Mike made the impressive Colony Trail building in less than 10 minutes via the Perry Walkway and made it up to the 11th floor, which was his father's office and laboratory.

The floor was deserted. That was not unusual in itself. The light was on in the office and the door was open. Light spilled out of the open office door cutting a swathe of white light across the dark floor.

As he got to the door, Mike froze. There was a putrid smell like bad eggs but much worse coming from the room. As he looked around the open door, his worst nightmare was confirmed. Despite its visored strong box, designed to house the host's eyes and essence during replication, his father's device had been deliberately smashed. The yellow ooze now staining the Persian rug was the source of the smell. Mike collapsed to the floor on his knees with the realisation that his dad was dead! No! Murdered!

Of the next few days, Mike could recall only snatched memories of events. The police, the family reunion, the funeral service, all merged into a blur of faces, feelings and emotions. Through all of that he carried one very strong feeling of anger and revenge, above all a passion, a determination to find the man who had done this and to exact a fitting retribution, in this case truly an eye for an eye!

"Mike! Mike! Are you OK? You're hyperventilating! Are you sick? What is it? You're burning up! Mike you're really scaring me now. Say something!"

Mike opened his eyes. He looked into Jaz's steel grey gaze and held for what seemed like an eternity.

"I'm just glad you're here with me right now." He whispered as he gently rubbed his chin against her forehead. "I've been so lonely without you Jaz, and now all this is driving me crazy. I need you so badly."

"Shussh now, it's OK" she said and led him gently by the hand to the cramped bunks.

CHAPTER FOUR: BREAKTHROUGH

"Mike! Mike! Wake up !"

Mike opened one eye and looked at Jasmine with a leer. "What! Again so soon?" he winked.

"Stop that now! No! Look, the Quorum team are waiting."

They got dressed quickly, the Quorum team waiting patiently at their consoles bowed in the customary acknowledgement of task completed. Mike studied their read-outs with avid interest.

"Looks like we've got something to work with here." he said. "Shall we try it?"

"OK, here goes nothing" she agreed.

"Right, let's get our gear together, full suits, plus spare oxygen modules each just in case."

Standing beside the blinking panel display, Mike lined up the improvised sensor array. Calibrating it to match the speed of the transmission, he co-ordinated the patterns internally until he was happy that the sequences were running in synch.

"Right, here goes" he said as he activated the transmit button. Nothing happened. They waited and looked at each other perplexed.

"What do you suppose....." Jasmine trailed off as the wall rippled before her, seemingly at the sound of her voice.

Mike tentatively reached out and touched the surface. It yielded to his touch with a sound something like a suction tube. An inch at a time, he extended his hand until it was completely immersed in the wall.

"It feels just like a very tight elastic wrapped around my hand, no pain, nothing, and quite warm to the touch. Here you try."

Jasmine put her hand into the surface and appeared to be surprised at the lack of resistance. She ventured further and immersed her arm fully to the elbow. Mike glanced anxiously at the "key" as it emitted a low whistle. When he looked back Jasmine was gone! The volume of the whistle increased to a shrill shriek. He made a split second decision and went through the wall himself turning as he went to see the translucent material on the inside of the wall close up like the iris of an eye to become solid rock again. As he walked backwards he tripped and fell heavily. Quickly back on his feet, he recognised with disbelief and concern Jasmine's discarded and abandoned pressure suit, but of her there was no sign. As he groped his way around in the semi darkness of the passage he knew there was no easy or obvious way out.

It seemed incongruous with Jasmine's discarded suit at his feet to remain suited himself, but as a precaution, he resisted the temptation to remove his own. Even though his gauges were indicating at least a thin atmosphere of breathable air, his mind kept telling him that it simply wasn't possible. Jasmine's fate was the more pressing problem at this moment however. Who or what had taken her, where and why? He had only questions and was desperate for some answers.

The low corridor he was in curved sharply to the right, which meant he would have to move along it if he wanted to see further. "This is madness," he said to himself, angry now at his foolhardiness, resigning himself to the grim fact that he had possibly destroyed any chance of rescue and survival by coming through the wall. With nothing to lose now, he determined to satisfy his own curiosity if for no other reason that he had had nothing else to do right now.

He took stock of his equipment and the suit's built-in survival kit. He tried the transmitter to the Quorum team and winced at the dull click he got in response. All the other standard issue items in the kit showed up positive icons in response to the check programme. The last item he checked was the one he hoped he wouldn't have to deploy, his standard issue laser sidearm. Under normal circumstances unnecessary weight, he'd often thought - now he was glad of is reassuring presence. He armed it now and put it back in place with the safety button on standby mode.

Checking out Jasmine's suit, he extracted all the goodies he could comfortably carry, including her weapon and set off toward the curve of the corridor. As he reached the turning point, he detected the by now familiar noise of the portal opening. Except that now it wasn't the one he'd just come through. He hurried around the bend to be confronted by a similar pulsating signal device some 20m away. Remembering how the outer door had suddenly closed down on him, he ran the remaining distance and without stopping dived head first through the viscous material and out the other side. As he went through he turned and observed the portal close in exactly the same way the outer one had. "An airlock, of course!" he realised. As if to confirm this, the oxygen reading on his wrist monitor soared to a "normal" breathable level and he felt normal gravity again.

"What is this?" he wondered to himself as he tentatively cracked open his helmet mounting and was surprised by the warm and pleasant atmosphere. 1,000 m beneath the surface of the Moon, breathing normally and standing in a "cavern" the size of a cathedral was the last thing he'd expected. Dim and concealed lighting from somewhere revealed his surroundings as devoid of any outstanding features of any kind. "Now what?" He decided to explore further. Any hopes of tracking down Jasmine seemed futile at this juncture. With no debris, no dust disturbance no signs of anything to suggest that she had even passed through this way he had no clue to give him a starting point. Surely she would have waited for him, or would have come back to check if he was OK if she could? IF SHE COULD! That thought hit him like a thunderbolt. What if she had been taken against her will, who or what had taken her and why? Had she been forcibly pulled through the portal? Had the portal been deliberately kept open for him? Had he just been incredibly lucky with the timing of the cycle? What else lay ahead for him to stumble across or deal with yet?

He sat down and took stock of his situation over a ration pack. His thoughts wandered back to a time long forgotten of him and Jasmine and their past together before the death of his father.

As far back as he could remember they had always been close friends, coming from the same commublock in uptown Hantsville in New Ameris State. They'd gone to school together then college, dated off and on through their teens, partied together and ran with the same crew of friends, life seemed to be one long party then.

As they had matured together into adulthood, their

affection and love for one another had embraced the romantic and passionate desires of the young. They were well matched. She was the intelligent beautiful and confident long legged blonde beauty with that sassy style; he with the dark handsome features, brown eyed and well toned body of the college athlete. They became an instant item, inseparable, causing less than a ripple of surprise amongst friends and family when they announced their engagement at the age of 19.

He was the son of the renowned and eminent innovator and inventor of Quorum Functionary Corporation, Professor Tom Brett. Whenever the man presented one of his discoveries to the world, it was always accompanied with his father's genuine attempts to improve the lot of his fellow man. The Quorum Team concept was such a typical example. He had hoped that by providing all nations with the means to free the masses once and for all from the drudgery of work through the duplication of manpower and thus the reduction in effort, a more cultured and less fraught society would emerge as a consequence. His deepest desire was to find the way to accelerate Man's appetite and quest for the opportunities he was convinced awaited them beyond the confines of their Earthly home, the stars and beyond!

He believed that by harnessing the best brains in the world, and literally multiplying their potential and applying the outcome to the known laws and parameters of physics, Man would find himself free to expand and explore the natural world around him and in the Universe as never before.

The real manifestation of that dream was evident here and now on the Moon where the embryonic exploration of space began to gather pace and the dream was to have become a brave reality and legacy for the generations to follow, thanks in no small way to the touches of genius with which the old man had been so generous. Richly rewarded too it had to be said, because in tandem with his creativity and imagination, Tom was a rare breed indeed, he was also a shrewd businessman.

Mike himself used his own skills well. Ensconced in his world of stellar engineering, in his own way, he was as passionate about his personal achievements as his father was about his. Well liked and respected by his colleagues and betters alike, Mike established a reputation as the best in his field and his skills were much sought after and well rewarded too. His idyllic lifestyle, flamboyant and always exciting, was all too easily shattered and destroyed by the gruesome and brutal death of the man he idolized.

He knew within himself that he had taken the death badly. Numbed with pain for weeks unending, he became morose and unapproachable. He retreated deeply within himself. Jasmine had the misfortune to bear the brunt of his grief. Ever supportive, she suffered every part of his hurt herself. Her father had been Tom's lifelong friend and his business partner, an alliance that had inevitably led to the momentum and means to initiate the Lunar project. Tom was the scientist and academic of the team; Rick Barson was the financial and commercial brain behind the operation. A no nonsense sometimes brutal ruthless mind in the corporate games scene, Rick had in large measure persuaded, bullied and cajoled, some even secretly hinted bribed, his own meteoric way to the very pinnacle of the business community. This manner was not to Mike's taste or sensibilities, but where Jasmine was concerned, he'd have been prepared to sell his own soul to have her by his side. So he tolerated the parts of Rick's nature he didn't like, his condescending manner, his loud voice, his tastes, assuring himself that his father was a better judge of character than he was.

He had come to realise, perhaps too late, that this faith in his old man's judgement was not well founded. There had been many heated and occasionally violent exchanges of views between the two men both at board meetings in public and in private "closed door" sessions. It soon became common knowledge and office gossip that the once impregnable fortress was showing signs of crumbling. Rick began to rely more and more on his own "men", amongst them the one Mike really took a dislike to from the outset, Paul Gregot. Seemingly from out of nowhere, Paul Gregot became Rick's right hand man, and the only one he would listen to and ask advice of. So the rift grew unchecked between the two families

Mike had been given most of his father's possessions after his death, his journals, diaries and the collection of recordings from his earliest achievements right up to the time of his murder. He was just coming to terms with that now. They were all there the failures as well as the successes, and they acquired a new meaning to him, as if they brought him closer somehow. Inevitably he would go over the mini disc collection whenever his duties allowed. The years of his growing up seemingly intertwined with the progress and success of the man and his work. It was on one such disc, one he had viewed numerous times that he had made a startling discovery. For some reason, perhaps an image on the screen, perhaps something that was said, reminded him that they had playfully agreed to a "secret" code between the two of them. It was a way of enabling the disc recording system in such a way that it allowed for the recording of an encoded encrypted message to be recorded on the outer rim of the disc. As he viewed each disc now, he consciously searched for their code. He found it on the 8th disc. The only discernible difference to the "normal" disc was that the opening titles would contain a few seconds of 20th century contemporary music. The music had always been a particular passion of Tom's.

He recalled the day of his discovery quite vividly.

Idling away another depressing day in silence, Jasmine had stormed off in frustration at his moods. As usual he turned to the discs for comfort and solace. He knew how badly he was hurting Jasmine yet he was unable to shake off his pain and anguish. He'd never been able to share his feelings very well before, and now she felt his rejection of her attempts to comfort him ever more keenly.

They had originally created the code as a joke when he was only 12. The fact that he'd stumbled across the boyhood toy on one of the most recently recorded discs, the last one completed just before his death, fascinated him yet sent shivers up and down his spine.

On first playing the message, he saw only his father as he was in the last few days of his life. The context of what he was saying and doing didn't register for at least 3 or 4 plays. As time began to diminish the sorrow, he began to really listen to what was being said and done. Long before Mike realised that adult deceit, double talk and hypocrisy were part and parcel of the adult world, the then youthful Tom had impressed upon the boy the importance of stealth, subterfuge and caution. As a scientist's discoveries were precious and rare commodities in a market only too willing to pay for short cuts by any means, Mike learned encryption almost as a religion, codes for everything were the norm and back up contingency plans became almost tedious chores whenever the two of them worked together.

He began picking up small signs at first. The finger code was the most obvious, but also the hardest to recall in all of its nuances. The message appeared to be quite open in nature. Tom revealed his concerns about developments at the highest commercial level of the company. He suggested that his suspicions pointed the finger at an unknown and unnamed executive in a position of great trust who was involved in underhand and sinister moves against their competitors. He stumbled across new technologies, which to all intents and purposes seemed to appear from nowhere, their origin clouded in vague explanations. Tom looked directly at the camera. " I know of at least two deaths directly linked to the operation of this company's policies. I am also fairly certain as to the identity of the people responsible. There is compelling and irrefutable evidence pointing to one individual on several counts of indictable actions. The very fact that you have discovered my message must mean I was right. I won't name him here and now for the safety of you and the rest of the family, my life I fear has already been the price for my discovery. There is for certain a very evil and catastrophic plan for the earth and its people, and I intend to stop it if I can. If I fail, the responsibility is yours Mike. This threat goes against everything we have ever stood for and makes a mockery of our ambitions for nothing more than personal greed and the lust for power at any cost."

At that point the message ended abruptly. No matter how hard he tried there was nothing more on this or on any of the remaining discs revealing anything more. It was obvious that Tom had uncovered a conspiracy within the organisation, which had wide-reaching implications. He had never seen his father so obviously rattled and afraid. It was only when he had played the message many times over that he began to pick up on the more subtle markers he'd only ever regarded with childish joy as a game. Now they were of utmost importance in his quest for knowledge and revenge. The finger code was confirmation that his office and lab were bugged, that his every word was being recorded and analysed. Aware that even their simple secret code was at risk, Tom was using a second code of eye movement at the same time, more sophisticated and hard for him to recall. When he'd remembered enough to make sense of the message, one name became a constant repetition. This Tom confirmed as his prime suspect with an overt virtual thumbs up. Even when he was 100% sure he had interpreted the message correctly, he wouldn't trust himself to believe it was true. Over and over he played the message until finally there was no room for any doubt. Even so without the hard evidence to support it, the suspicion was just that.

The more he viewed the disc, the more he would find himself picking up on small unconnected clues and anomalies. With a great effort of will, he ignored the image of Tom as the focus of his attention and played closer attention to the area immediately around the desk. The monitor to Toms left reflected the smallest movement towards the end of the message. From the angle of the screen he guessed that it had come from a glass panel set into the natural oak door to the office. His father insisted on everything around him being as natural as possible. The fleeting image proved to be unusable; he could not enhance the image beyond an indistinct blob. He noticed something that didn't seem right on the panels of active hardware along the back wall. This represented the nerve centre of the prototype Quorum process. On the scanner device, one small portion of the stasis field remained stubbornly unlit at each sweep of the beam. At the first opportunity he'd gone back to the office once the police investigation was over. Feigning a need to be amongst his father's possessions, he found and removed what seemed to be a microscopic dot from the screen. He discovered its purpose was common in espionage circles, a recording device, but this particular one was of unknown origin. The investigation had concluded death by misadventure, an experiment too far, untried equipment or equipment failure. Mike knew otherwise but was powerless to act without the hard evidence to support his claim - so he kept quiet, knowing his moment would come soon enough. When the sensationalism of the incident had subsided and the investigation was wound up, media interest and concern predictably diverted its attentions elsewhere. Mike confronted Rick with what he knew. Incredibly, Rick had just laughed in his face. That had been one insult too far for Mike; his attack on Rick would have been far more serious had it not been for the intervention of his right hand man, Paul Gregot. Seemingly never far from Rick's side these days, Paul was proving to be something of a genius within the corporation, and definitely Rick's "blue eyed boy". With an I.Q. several bands above his father's, he was also physically formidable, a deadly combination. Even so Mick stood his ground, toe to toe with Rick, and vowed to expose his and Paul's calculated and perverse bastardisation of the company for their own purposes, and with it their lust for control of Man's very destiny.

Rick had coolly challenged him to prove anything he could, before turning back to face him and showed a side of himself rarely if ever exposed in public. The cold blooded monster he was so often accused of being reared its ugly head as he spelled out in no uncertain terms the depth of the contempt he felt for Mike's idealistic view of Tom and all he stood for. Before he had Paul eject him from the building, he vowed to ruin him, kick him out of the company, or worse.

True to his word, surrounded as he was by the most powerful lawyers his money and position commanded, Mike's interest and influence within the Visage Corporation Industries was systematically dismantled, like the fingers of a hand being forcibly removed from a treasured possession. Rick stole his birthright from him as he had promised he would. With nothing to hold on to, Mike was cut adrift.

Naturally his relationship with Jasmine came under enormous strain. She adored her father, as much as Mike admired his own. She would hear no ill spoken of him. Row upon row left them emotionally drained and strained, pushing them further and further apart until Mike realised that this was also evidence of the damage Rick was capable of. Of all men, he had to lose her to him. At that point he felt only too acutely the bitter after-taste of defeat at the hand of a master, but there was no way he would let it lie. He would have his day.

He had little problem in re-establishing his engineering career. He took most of his crew with him and set up in his own right with the best, most skilled and experienced space-engineering outfit anywhere on Earth. Even the irony of having to lease the Quorum technology from the very corporation he had spent his entire life being a part of didn't detract from the plain fact that Earth needed his specific skills and experience at this most crucial stage of it's quest for the stars. His contacts and lifelong friends outside of the Corporation ensured his continued involvement in the pursuit of Tom's dream, rapidly now becoming his own. Always but always now he made sure to cover his back mindful that ultimately, he still had to deal with Rick at the end of the day. At least he comforted himself with the fact that he had him where he could keep an eye on him. Yes, he could afford to wait for the right moment.

And so he had found himself here on the Moon, a vital player in the global effort to give mankind its first stepping stone on its long and eventful journey through and beyond the cosmos. Little did he realise at the time that this soon in their journey they would face the evidence that previous travellers had been there before them. This last thought was a fresh one added to his knowledge and experience of the adventure so far.

He re-played the message now as he sat alone in the dim light of the huge cavern. He always carried the tape collection with him wherever he went. As he keyed in his eye visor viewer, he started in amazement as the playback went beyond the message he knew by heart. The view screen flared briefly and a new recording carried on beyond the end of the usual end of message signal. In this part of the message, he was looking at the Quorum bank at the far end of his father's office, and very specifically at Tom's personal containment unit. He started again as Tom's whispered words came through. "Mike, if you are hearing this then I am dead for sure. I set the device to trigger on the 500th viewing to be sure that only you would find it. There is one point of weakness in my security system when I can be vulnerable to danger, the Quorum tank itself. Ironic isn't it? Keep watching this and you will have the necessary evidence to commit the man I strongly suspect to justice. Goodbye son! You will know the right thing to do. I love you!"

Mike sat spellbound by the unexpected message. He flicked the viewer to fast forward, slowing it to normal speed when the scene of the empty office changed. He witnessed the most subtle and calculated piece of pure evil he had ever witnessed. He knew that at that time the Quorum process had required the donor to "convalesce" for up to 6 hours after decommissioning, before they emerged from its process as if from a deep sleep. Until a few minutes before recovery, the body remained unsubstantial apart from the eyes themselves, which retained their solid from throughout the process. As a humorous quirk, Tom had designed the containment tank in such a way that the eyes observed their surroundings through a viewing port. In this condition, they continued to function as normal, so he knew with some pain and distress, that Tom had watched helpless as his killer corrupted the restoration process by simply bleeding off static from the containment field. The effect was almost instantaneous as the helpless eyes first visibly yellowed and then seemed to shrivel as the vital fluids boiled and breached the delicate seals keeping them in place. As the assassin turned to leave, the secret recorder printed up the unmistakeable recognition code leaving no room for doubt as to the killer's identity

Fully 10 minutes elapsed before he could force himself to acknowledge the enormity of this latest development. Unable to move, think or feel anything, Mike struggled with this unexpected twist of the knife in his side. With the horrible moments of death now etched it seemed permanently on the back of his eyeballs, the tears flowed unchecked as once again he rode the roller-coaster of sheer despair, anger, frustration and now a renewed feeling of revenge and retribution. With a great effort of will he forced himself to be focused clearly now, he constructively directed his thoughts to his prime target. No doubt, there would be a dear price to pay indeed!

To this controlled aggression, he now added the emotional anguish of Jasmine's disappearance from his side, for a second time. This time he would not let her go so easily. He desperately needed a plan, but what could he do? Cut off from any outside help in an alien environment and facing unknown odds. He smiled at the seeming helplessness of it all. 'This time they won't stop me' he thought. Instinct told him that Rick and Paul were heavily involved in whatever was going on here too. He did not know how that was or how it had come to be, he just knew it for a fact. Now was the time for some clear thinking and plotting of his own. With calm assurance he cleared his head of all thoughts and willed himself to fully relax, He sensed rather than felt the tensions in his body drain away as he entered the world of his inner consciousness and sought the refuge as he had so many times since Jasmine left him that dark brooding night when she finally gave up on his black moods and drunken squalor. Only this time instead of solace and comfort, he sought out a much deeper purpose. With effortless ease a new clarity of thought seemed to guide him through the tortured facts of his recent life, giving him finally a strategic and purposeful solution to the problem. Refreshed and alert he returned to full consciousness and set about preparing his next move.

CHAPTER FIVE: CONTACT

Bhodran's face creased into a scowl. He felt as though he'd been doing that a lot lately. Nothing seemed to make much sense these last few days, especially now as he approached the end of his "Woken". He felt as though his five years had been futile and wasted. To have studied and learned so much only now to have to make way for somebody else seemed so stupid. And he felt resentful too! Who decided the lifespan anyway? He knew the dynamics of their existence of course. The eco-structure of their world would support only one million beings at any one time. There were over 100 million beings in the bands above his head. They were each allowed three years before returning to their icy beds where they slept in suspension for another ten thousand years before their turn for resurrection came round again. This was only his first re-awakening since their arrival at the planet. He had matured into adulthood in this Woken, and he wondered at all the discoveries and changes he would miss until the next time. Even though he knew in conscious terms it would feel as though he had spent a night in heavy sleep, he could not help but feel the frustration of so many years passing him by from this point. Certainly not since his "education" at the hands of his Master.

He leaned back into his support module and casually

summarised the events of the last few days. He could pinpoint the start of his uneasiness to the discovery of an anomaly in the usually boring but compulsory readings of the "Globeye". The most revered artefact of their history on this world, the "Globeye" contained the heritage of his entire race. He was especially privileged to have access to it. Very few of his kind were ever allowed anywhere near its complex setting deep within a secured compartment three levels below the floor of the Sciences Dome. Everybody was aware of it and it's contents of course, each one indoctrinated from birth and their knowledge reinforced at each Woken. But he should have felt privileged to be allowed such close access. Without thinking he automatically began reciting the litany of the law, almost as if he would find a clue to this dilemma, something he'd overlooked or misinterpreted perhaps.

"The Supreme is all knowing"

"The Way is Eternally Forward"

"The Return is Unseeing"

"The Future Guides Our Past"

"Home is at the Heart"

He found little solace in this summation of the Faith of their Race, but a feeling of tranquillity pervaded his thoughts now as he calmed his tormented thoughts into the fatalistic nature of their reality on this inadequate planet.

As he gazed upwards and outwards, through the curved protection of the bronze coloured dome, beyond the precariously thin membrane of breathable atmosphere and out into the field of brilliant stars, he soundlessly formed the urgent questions in his head "Who are we and Why?" The stars, eternal enigmas and puzzles were quite likely to provide the answers they all sought now, especially so in the aftermath of his shattering and frightening discovery. All of their beliefs were now open to scrutiny and challenge as never before. Novadon, his world, his existence, its laws and its myths were about to be exposed as a sham and a cover for the truth, whatever that really was. He had already reconciled himself with the fact that all of his earlier education and teachings had been a façade, a cover-up of the true story of their arrival on this planet. If the rest of the population knew what he now knew, it was more than likely that they would rise up and revolt.

The history of Novadon was dominated by accounts of a disaster of fantastic proportions on a planet like Novadon but much bigger and very different from the existence he now endured. On the other Novadon, the population of multi millions was free to exist and populate their world at will. Not like their own restrictive and fanatically enforced maximum of 100 births per year. There birth occurred freely and unchecked, unregulated. Instead of the controlled periods of Woken, here, citizens in that existence enjoyed unlimited and uninterrupted life-spans of at least 70 years each, some people having as many as three or four life-spans if he had interpreted the texts correctly. Not for them the deprivation of 3 years work then hibernation!

On one of his customary watches of the first quarter, when he had entered the study-room for his reflect-time, he had initialised the visi-sequencer as always. In place of the usual screen response, a new signal had appeared. In the visible light spectrum, a warning device of unknown origin to him glowed ominously on the screen where he would normally see the beginning of his Master's Mantra. He checked and re-checked the controls after referring to every section of the manual he could think of with no response. In the end he had concluded that he had no alternative but to arouse his appointed mentor from his private quarters, not an undertaking he relished at all. The elders were highly protective of their private time. Whoever had the temerity to disturb them during this time either had to be in mortal danger or have a convincing reason for their actions.

When he had activated and reactivated Shedratt's pod, he had been prepared for a string of abusive language, as was the Master's nature. But once appraised of the cause of his interruption, Shadratt had been lavish in his praise of the younger man. Everything then seemed to dissolve into a frenzy of activity within the walls of this normally calm and monastic building of study, reflection and learning. Starting with Shedratt's personal reading of the signal at his station, the resulting pandemonium of top level officials and officers being roused and briefed seemed to go on for days, almost is if they feared the domes themselves were about to come crashing in at any minute.

And now as he stood his last few watches before his Downzone he felt deep envy and anxiety that it would fall to his successor to enjoy all the excitement of the discovery in his place. He had to consciously repress his feelings of despair and anger at the unfairness of his position as for the umpteenth time he rationalised his sacrifice against the greater good of his race. He was sad that even though his next Woken period would give him all the answers he sought, it would once again be ancient history to him.

For many tens of thousands of years now his people had endured the necessity of these recurring cycles to give them some semblance of a purposeful existence. History told of their being cast out from the perfection that was their true home Terrania. This had been the work of one they referred to as the Universal Evil. This one being had angered their Creator by daring to challenge His very wisdom. Their fate then had been to be cast off into space in their ships and banished from the beauty of their old world to search for a refuge, a copy of their old home somewhere in the vast void of space. This exile had forged in them the habit of regular short-life/ long-sleep until finally they had reached the given co-ordinates of their new "home".

Unlike the prophecies of the land of plenty and abundance, as they approached their promised land, their scientists were horrified to discover a planet that seemed to mock them with each day as they neared its position. In appearance and in composition it was indeed similar to their Old World. It was tragically the scale of the planet that proved to be the centre of the calamity. This planet was smaller than Terrania by a factor of 10. Worse than that, the atmosphere was thinner than that on Terrania and extended a mere 2 metres above the surface of the planet. To come to this place in place of the fabled golden land of plenty was to say the least a universal shock. No amount of frantic scouring of the surrounding emptiness yielded the slightest possibility of an alternative. They had committed everything to attain this position, they were stuck now and had to make the best they could whilst they set to work to salvage their people's fate.

Emergency council had been called while the two million space ships were manoeuvred into orbit above the planet. Their leaders had been brought out of their cryogenic sleep and lengthy debate on the best means of survival raged for over a decade whilst the people themselves, 10,000 per ship, slept on unaware of their precarious position. Bodrahn could see the circles of silver above him now as their sun broke the horizon over to his left. Four bands, each one four ships wide and ten deep made for a spectacular sight. The hidden tragedy was, that apart from the Grand Awakening when they had all been raised from their induced sleep to be informed of their fate and assigned their time slots, that at any one time 90% of their population was in enforced repose. Lately there had been many debates regarding the stability of the generating units and the long-term effects of such a situation on the physical well being of humans to add to their misery. The people had taken the news remarkably well with just the merest hint of rebellion when a group of 100 ships had fought for and been granted the right to break away and search beyond their known space for a better world. They had been granted their wish, taking a proportion of the precious supplies brought from Terrania and the anxious wishes of the fellow travellers for good luck. Following their departure, the construction ships had landed on the planet surface to begin the arduous and almost impossible task of providing a safe and habitable environment for the people. From the outset it became obvious that the restrictions of land area and natural resources, water, vegetation construction materials, meant that they could not disembark the entire fleet of ships ever. So they had created their unnatural existence of the 'cycles. The age of the Engineers had dawned and reigned supreme for many millennia.

The Engineers made up over a quarter of the Ruling Council in the beginning. Their kind was selectively awoken for their very specific skills and disciplines. First they created the domes which now covered over 25% of the available solid mass of Novadom. Each dome was the metropolis for over 100,000 people, self sufficient in oxygen, water and food production. Within the area enclosed by the dome, the process of terra-forming would begin with the object of adding to the atmosphere of the planet by photosynthesis. The higher the level of the oxygen level, the more land would become available to them in the high land areas of the planet, now devoid of any breathable atmosphere, at least another two thirds of the planet area. The only down side to the plan was the pace of development. Not having anticipated the problem of the scale of the planet, their equipment was heavily weighted in favour of metal forming technology. Even with the combined inventory of all the engineering class ships, their terra-forming equipment was the equivalent of only one Terran class machine back home. Progress was guaranteed to be excruciatingly slow.

The Cycles had originally been a temporary measure. Every three years one of the orbiting ships was brought to land and the passengers revived for their period of Woken. Those designated for Downzone replaced the new arrivals in the cryogenic pods and the ship returned to its former orbit. Offspring were kept on the surface in the Crechedome until they reached the age of 16 years. Then they too took their place in the Cycles. During the first 50 years, the Engineers were the only class to be exempt from the Cycles, because of the nature of their skills and knowledge. They found an abundance of volunteers willing to acquire their skills and knowledge, not merely to assist in the colonisation but also as a means of avoiding enforced unconsciousness. It was a routine now which prevailed as a permanent feature of the life on Novadon. The only comfort was that the scale of the consequences of their primary error in miscalculating the eco-system of this world was that for the vast majority of sleepers, until their period of Woken came around, they were none the wiser. Once they were awoken to the reality, almost from their first day, they were counselled in preparation for their return.

Although this was Bhodran's first session since arrival, he was appalled at the lack of progress made against his expectations. Very little on the global scale had changed. Yes they had colonised vast tracts of land, yes they were disembarking five ships at a time now, yes they had developed a new propulsion system for the ships with greater capabilities, and yes, domestic comforts were increasing in sophistication. Yet he could not help the feeling that there was no urgency to progress beyond this "maintenance" mode. Their technology resource was severely limited of course by that which they had brought with them. Apparently the mineral content of this world left them with very little new material to generate machines big enough to alter the quality and quantity of oxygen with any degree of significance. The agricultural programme was limited by the extent of freedom of movement outside of the domes, which was inhibited by the lack of oxygen, and so they were themselves subject to a cruel pattern of "cycles". Since his Downzone began, the oxygen content had increased by a mere 0.7%, and the layer extended a mere 3 metres above the surface. An ozone layer was beginning to thicken up now above the oxygen layer, but it was all relative to the pace of industrialisation on the surface.

His personal thoughts he kept to himself, as much to avoid the questions about his commitment to their cause to a minimum. The committee would just as soon take away his privileged status if they thought he showed any negative attitude to their situation. He valued his status, giving him access to study facilities and extra comforts beyond the ordinary citizen, his extra two years Woken time for one. For all the perception of continuity in ones life, the cryogenic existence affected his psychological balance extremely hard. He was aware of the many whispered reports of suicides amongst the Woken. No doubt this in part explained why they were unloading more ships at one time now than earlier. The current "going" rate was about 2000 people who in the first month of re-awakening would kill themselves in despair. The pattern of deaths suggested a greater prevalence of suicide in the lower skills social groups. The Government was secretly very worried. They recognised that the pace of their technological advances was insufficient to keep pace with the growing expectations of successive waves of colonists and there was always the threat of revolt and anarchy if they lost control of the discipline of the Cycles.

And now there was the "message". With it his world was about to be totally transformed for reasons he did not yet appreciate. As he looked around again to his right he could see the twenty fleet cutters of the Governors of the continents. In all they had brought together 500 of their most eminent engineers and 300 of the Scientist community. They were gathering in the Grand Hall, one of their few triumphs of technology against the elements. It stood 30 metres tall, towering over the surrounding domes. Unlike the domes it was open to the atmosphere at the top, its precious life support system held in check by a force field. He, yes he Bhodran, had been called to give this assembly his first hand account of the receiving of the message. They were awaiting the arrival of further important guests hastily retrieved from the circling Belts of Dhor, as they had named the orbiting craft. The best minds of scholastic, intellectual and professional sects were going to interpret his report and make far-reaching decisions on what he had to say. He didn't know whether to be nervous or thrilled so he decided on neither and merely accepted that this as to be his parting gift to his fellow scholars.

In little more than an hour, he had been summoned and now stood before the Assembly, elated and proud. He marvelled at the sight of the heavens above them, seeing them for the first time without the bronze barrier of the dome. They sparkled bright and silver against the solid blackness. Although he remembered the stars from Terrania, he could not recall them being as clear and spectacular as these. The atmosphere tasted different too. They had installed a much more efficient oxygen plant here, recycling and enhancing the natural atmosphere of the Hall itself instead of the usual replicator systems used elsewhere. He was ushered through a series of imposing stone doorways before finally arriving at the bottom of a circular amphitheatre. The tiers of seats rose high above him giving all those assembled a clear view of the podium itself. The arrangement also made direct communication with each other more comfortable, as each of the kiosks was able to extend itself forward when its occupants were called upon to speak. He had arrived during a briefing of the Space Engineers on further advances made on the propulsion systems for the ships. Why that was important he couldn't work out, they had nowhere to go! Someone was finishing a presentation on the Hargon System of faster-than-light travel.

The next speaker presented a disturbing presentation on advances with weaponry. Bhodran had not been aware that such research was being done, further consternation for him as he recognised that the theme was not defensive, but offensive and aggressive weapons. He began to have doubts about the consequences of his revelation but before he could crystallise his thoughts he was called forward to the podium to speak.

His sponsor had ensured that he was well versed in the necessary protocols in addressing the Assembly of the Council. With little evidence of nerves, Bhodran proceeded to deliver his report. He gave them his account of the circumstances before, during and since his discovery of the "anomaly" of his research findings and the interpretation he had put upon the encrypted message. He described how he had applied the use of his portable visi-screen, the crowning glory of his graduation into the science class, to make sense of the ancient wording in the message. Calmly and with supreme confidence he presented his summation of the probability factors of pinpointing its point of origin. It was only when he had completed his polished presentation and switched off the visual aid equipment that he became aware of the total and deafening silence in the auditorium.

The leader of the Council, Estravon, broke the silence, anxious to dispel the young man's trepidation.

"Thank you Bhodran for your eloquent and succinct appraisal of these facts."

Bhodran relaxed a little.

"Do you appreciate the TRUE significance of this information?" he continued

"No Minister, I am not yet fully qualified enough in the ancient writings to put any interpretation on the readings provided by this transmission. My sole aim was to accurately interpret the content so that others more qualified than myself could do so."

"You have done extremely well!" smiled Estrovan, genuinely pleased with the way in which Bhodran had presented his findings.

"Garvoran, if you please." Estrovan invited the Senior Science Councillor to take his position at the podium.

"Thank you Minister. Bhodran, please be seated. You have earned the right to hear our conclusions. Gentlemen, be prepared, for what you are about to hear heralds the fulfilment of our wildest dreams...... the return to Terrania!"

Slowly at first, then travelling like a wave of sound the entire assembly erupted into a babble of demands for clarification and details. Garvoran stood impassively, waiting for the noise to diminish into a buzz of subdued conversations and the occasional cry of concern from one quarter or another before resuming his position. Silence descended at once.

"The message contains data, in my belief deliberately erased from our archive of records, concerning the path we followed in our quest to reach this the New World of Novadon. Without that vital data, plans for any possibility of retracing our journey of exile were doomed to failure. We think this was part of the punishment of banishment placed upon us. Our venerated Scientists have now confirmed that the encryption codes contained within the message received by Bhodran, have revealed to us the location of a sacred tabernacle, a relic from the Old World. Our forefathers entrusted this relic to us. Protected by our Theoligist Sect, this trust was absolute and irrefutable until and unless they received a sign, known to them alone, which released them from their guardianship of this knowledge. The account given by Bhodran here of the receipt of this message was coincidental and linked to the activation of the protective shield of the tabernacle itself. For many years, many scholars and students alike have endeavoured to unlock its mysteries with no success. The message activated a chronometer driven locking mechanism operated from within, which opened the tabernacle itself. What was found inside the tabernacle we have been instructed to apply to the text of the message. Within that message lies the entire portion of "lost" knowledge of the history of our race, so vast that we are still placing its data upon our computers now as we speak. It gives us so much more knowledge than that which we had before. But perhaps of greatest significance is that we have a clear picture now of the origin of our flight and the circumstances of its execution. This message contradicts much of our belief in the manner of our banishment. Were we not told that because of our excesses we faced the obliteration of our world? Were we not told we were to flee for fear of annihilation of our race? The very existence of this message exposes those exaltations as lies! Our world prevailed, our species survived and our banishment amounts to nothing more than genocide on an impossible scale. Who is to say that we were not "evicted" from Terrania by some intelligent race envious of our world. Our existence here proves that they held scant regard for our survival. Gentlemen, the time has come for me to invoke the powers latently invested in me to call for ....A COUNCIL OF WAR!"

Bhodran was taken aback in horror. He had imagined a purely theological approach in the appraisal of his discovery. Perhaps he had been in hybersleep for so long, he had not been exposed to the growing feeling of resentment at their plight. But he could not sit by now and allow these leaders to turn his triumph into something ugly and unthinkable. He realised he had no other option but to give them his unproven and untried second findings.

He claimed his position on the Speakers Point and cleared his throat.

"Venerated Members of the Council," he began hesitantly. "This message could have been an automatic device, activated at a certain point in time when the threat to the Old World had passed or when conditions on the planet returned to normal. I have further transmissions from an earlier date which indicate such an eventuality took place. The reason I have not disclosed this to you was that I had not yet completed the necessary fault seeker sequence to authenticate my conclusions. The unqualified transcript tells of an unstoppable and unseen force of nature which overwhelmed the entire planet, destroying all living matter in its path, erasing all evidence of intelligent life and civilisation in its path. The advent of this event was predicted and it was this prediction which prompted the Scientists to create a means of survival for our people. Their answer was the discovery of this planet which was believed to be close to the same composition as Terrania , sufficient to cater for our needs. They could not know from such a great distance the reality of what we encountered on our arrival to be the true picture. To them it represented the only choice, that or die! The reading also talks of alternative experiments with a device for deflecting the onslaught of this event, and that one man stood alone in his quest to find a better solution, but he was largely ignored, passed over in the rush to prepare our people for exodus into space. He is mentioned only once, and almost dismissed as a crank and a dreamer. This man, named only as Dhoran, elected to remain behind to prove his beliefs. In the final parting he is quoted as saying that if his quest to save our planet were successful, that he would send a pre-arranged sequence of signals which would recall the fleet. We know that no such signal was received and our exodus was confirmed. Let me show you the last moments of our departure as seen from our Old World." From the lectern, Bhodran opened up the holographic display. It showed the departure of the last of the fleet, then panned back to Terrania showing its transformation from the beautiful blue and white marbled globe to a dead and ugly looking ball of grey nothingness.

"Is it not conceivable that this could also be part of the propaganda designed to keep us on our course of exodus, to force us to continue our journey and forget our old way? Who is not to say that the 1000 ships found missing when we emerged here at the end of our journey were not lost as we feared through mishap, but returned to the planet and claimed dominion. The entire 1000 ships were all "G" class vessels, carrying a select group of citizens of the Ruling class. They are unaccounted for to this day." This came from one of the higher tiers well above Bhodran's vision temporarily blinded by the lighting.

"Venerated member for Domain 35, your comment is well put. However, let us act in orderly fashion." Govran acknowledged the concern he knew would be shared by many seeing and hearing this part of the transmission for the first time. He himself wanted to examine this new development for himself before precipitating any further action.

Bhodran had not considered the scenario painted as a possibility, but he had to concede the point. Sometime during their long journey to Novadon, a thousand vessels had vanished from the monitors on the automated systems controlling their flight during the long sleep. Only when they had all been reactivated on their arrival had the loss been discovered. At the time, more pressing needs had meant scant attention being paid to the disappearance. They would certainly want to re-examine the ship's data banks now in the light of these revelations.

"Furthermore," continued the voice he now recognised as the Chief of Staff for the Fleet, "we now have the means and the ability to return to our true home-world in a fraction of the time it took us to arrive here. Days in fact! Since the successful conversions of the standard ships and the latest test results, we could have the entire fleet ready within 8 weeks, but only if we take the decision now to bring all our people back. Think! We could be reclaiming our rightful heritage in a few weeks time! Is that not a better proposition than this excuse of a part-time life?"

Once again the acoustics of the Grand Hall echoed to the sound of the multitude of questions and comments aimed at the Higher Command.

The Minister called the assembly back to order again. He called for a consensus of action. The conclusion they reached was the preparation of an advance fleet of 2000 vessels. They were to be fitted with the recent engine modifications and all would be modified with the weapons also developed. Only military personnel would be re-awoken to crew them with the intention of reconnaissance to begin with, and recapture of Terrania, by force if necessary. He then turned his attention to Bhodran once more.

"Bhodran, I have studied your background with interest. Of all our young scientists, you alone have proven to be a scholar of exceptional ability. Your skills in this quest as a student of the ancient cultures and your newly acquired knowledge of the Old World will be invaluable to us. You will join me on my flagship, to be known as The Phalanx as

First Science Officer and Personal Aide. Your designated Downzone is hereby cancelled indefinitely." He smiled and paused for a second. "Who knows, perhaps we will be able to afford this privilege to all of our people. It is decided then. We depart in 8 weeks time. Go and prepare your ships!"

With that the conference concluded. In the flurry of activity that followed, Bhodran never got the chance to reveal his third and final piece of knowledge. He had had an earlier signal which he had left unexplored. He had not thought to examine it because at the time, his level of competence had not allowed him access to the decoding machines in the main Science Dome. He had much work to do to get ready for this new assignment whilst the preparations went ahead and he left it for a later time, promptly forgetting all about it in the excitement and tension all around him.

CHAPTER SIX: REVELATION

Finally the small craft began to inch its way above the now upward and outward bound lunar surface. Reaching the edge, Jack rolled the ship over, and was relieved to see the Moon still within range below him. Without the benefit of the small gravitational pull of his magno-grab, the craft fell into a gentle free fall affording him a unique view of the unfolding scene above. Four separate segments of displaced moon surface were drifting in the opposite direction. They had each begun to break up, yet still retained the almost comical impression of floating segments of an orange until, looking down towards the main surface, the results were anything but a joke! It appeared as though a huge slice of the normally white gleaming familiar and friendly face of the moon had been ripped away revealing a dark and ugly scarred remnant in its place; threatening almost in its new appearance.

With a sigh of relief, he realised that the ship was finally beginning to respond to his command. He tuned in and homed in on the home base beacon, not afraid to admit that the last few hours had been traumatically scary to say the least. Although he would never admit it to anyone but himself, he was petrified at the scale of events taking place. He'd joined the company only six months previous, straight out of the tech academy, and this had been his first assignment, his dream realised. After two weeks intensive training and competition, he had qualified as the best of his class, the coveted space engineering apprenticeship was his reward. From early days as a child even he felt his destiny was to be amongst the unstoppable movement of people and resources towards and beyond the skies and stars. And now here it was. Reality!

The events of the last few days had shocked and tested his nerve severely. He sensed that they had also matured him in some way and given him an alternative perspective on his attitudes towards his responsibilities. In earlier times, he himself knew he would have cracked up, run away, or hidden to avoid anything threatening or remotely as challenging as this. Despite his well-polished image during his student years as a cool head in adverse moments, truth-be-known, he knew himself to be a coward at heart. Until now that was! Here and now was his true test. He felt sure of his place here, he knew what was expected of him, what he expected of himself. His resolve had been sorely tried for sure but here he was and finally out here alone and in trouble, he knew the moment of truth had arrived for Jack Kidd.

He had waited, watched and listened as drama after drama unfolded before him. Out of the blue the destruction of the moon base colony had been like a hammer blow. Even now he was unable to correlate 2000 lives with the disappearance of the dome, the scale of the loss of life incomprehensible to him, Christ, he didn't even know that he had even met that many people in his life yet!

He didn't even kid himself that he was regarded as anything out of the ordinary. He knew he had been assigned to "Ship Watch", about as non-responsible a duty as you could get in engineering. There was no glory in that, yet he did not begrudge Mike, his boss and superior officer leading the way in exploring the most obvious manifestation of the disaster, the rift. Even knowing what his role would be, he had volunteered instantly when asked. Now, it was his turn to return the confidence shown in his abilities and character. When the second readings of seismic activity had appeared on the screens, he had followed protocol to the letter, advising first home base of the situation, and then the away teams. He then braced himself for the severe shaking that would inevitably follow, but had not expected to be shaken off the surface in such a dramatic manner! In the flurry of activity seconds before abandoning the 'Streak, he had set the auto-return control and activated it in the vain hope that there might be a chance for the ship to make it back to base. It had been touch and go, only Mike's timely advice had prevented further disaster and saved his bacon yet again.

The unfriendly lunar visage was growing in his monitors and filling the visor of the craft. Try as he might, he could see no logic to the whole thing. The separation of the surface, segmented, an imperfect orb, to what end, what purpose, and why? An entire array of convoluted questions and thoughts raced each other across his imagination. His only concern and primary question now was what had become of Mike and Jasmine? He had tracked their every move up to the point of their descent and discovery of the portal at which point all his sensors blanked out apart from the vital signs readouts, indicating the continuing presence of the crew in the depths of the ravine. The final garbled transmission had been a life-saver for sure, but strange that final contact had been re-established at that most vital moment. Now, fully in command again, and with renewed optimism for his own survival, he methodically checked and activated the instruments and recording devices in a determination to provide as many clues for the ground boys to analyse as he neared his targeted point of trajectory and set course for the home base.

Once he was within range, he calmly made radio contact, reporting concisely and accurately the events leading up to and since the disappearance of Mike and Jasmine. Of the other teams there was no word, rescue teams were already out and looking but it didn't sound too encouraging. They had all witnessed the latest development in the most graphic manner, the evidence was there in front of them, a new spectacle in the lunar sky. Communication with Earth was still problematical since the first disaster with so many satellites out of commission or destroyed. But now, those that were still functioning were practically glowing with the weight of communications traffic demanding updates and visual confirmations from possibly every department and agency involved in space explorations, not to mention the journalist hackers who made it through inevitably. "Just make sure you make it back in one piece Jack!" he heard in a genuine plea of concern in the sign off message from his contact at base. He recognised her as Vikky Onlet, a small dark-haired communications expert who'd joined the team around the same time as he had. She was pretty, but seemed to be somewhat aloof towards him until now, maybe he'd misjudged her. So she had been moved up two notches too he mused. Everybody still here was expected to assume greater responsibility whilst the Earth rescue mission got into gear.

"Just what the hell is going on?" demanded Jasmine. "Who's brilliant idea was it to initiate Phase 3?" her eyes were blazing and she adopted her usual 'I-don't-take-no-for-an-answer' stance .

The creature standing in front of her was well over 6 feet tall, totally encased from head to foot in a shining suit of seamless black material, the black visor over the face reflecting her hostile attitude back down at her. He seemed just as unmoved and un-moveable as she herself until with a deafening roar of laughter it reached up and removed the visor to reveal the laughing face of her father underneath.

" Jasmine, Jasmine, you look as lovely as ever!" he seemed to boom " and angry as hell too by the looks of it, as usual."

"Cut the bullshit! I nearly died out there dammit!" she yelled back "and 2000 others did lose their lives! That was never mentioned to me either, how could you allow that?

"Hey, hey, honey! It's alright, slowly now it's OK, it's OK." said her father as he reached out a comforting hand. He flinched as she pushed it away and turned away from him. His smile disappeared.

"We got most of the personnel in containment centres before it hit. Only those unfortunate to be on the surface perished......."

Jasmine turned on him and unleashed the wildest string of expletives he had ever heard anywhere, let alone from the mouth of his own daughter.

"No-one was to be harmed, no-one! Don't you see what the difference is here? You've destroyed everything! You're a.... a.... a.... killer......!"

As soon as the words left her mouth, she realised her folly. Never before had she dared to challenge her father. She had been loyal and faithful devoted to him since the death of her mother during her early teens. They had pledged to support and care for each other no matter what. He had been true to his pledge as had she. Always the devoted daughter, she had been proud to stand in for her mother whenever business protocols had called for the social niceties of a "hostess". She had quickly learned about the unseen face of commerce and became educated in the real ways of the business community below the "acceptable" face generally shown to the public, to the point where she was able to match her father's undoubted prowess in the board room strategy wars. Her skill was much more subtle in both its creation and execution to the point that when the hard nosed brash and sometimes brutal approach failed to secure his ambitions, Rick thought nothing of unleashing her sharp and agile business mind on an unsuspecting client. Success was always guaranteed! Together they made a formidable team. He always thought that her talents were wasted when she chose to pursue a career in sciences rather than join him in business.

When it had come to a choice between her father and her marriage to Mike, without hesitation she had sided with her father. Mike had made the mistake of daring to challenge him, her rock, her life. It had been no contest. The way Mike had behaved at the time, accusing Rick of murder, the murder of Mike's father, had been so out of character that she could not forgive him this transgression. Now all that she had blindly believed in was thrown up for questioning. She herself began to buckle at the thought that she may, just may have misplaced her faith so badly. It was no longer an impossibility. She realised that with her rekindled love for Mike and her concern for his safety, there was a dangerous underlying current of conflict between Rick and herself threatening to surface and overwhelm her.

The blow she was expecting never came. She lowered her arms only to find him grinning at her from behind his desk.

"Boy, when you blow, you blow," he said "just like your mother."

His eyes hardened and it was back to business as usual.

"I agree, the programme shift has caused some unforeseen and unfortunate problems, and I do mean I regret the loss of lives. The end always justifies the means and the consequences are a matter of degree. Besides, we did not precipitate the disaster. It caught even us by surprise too. What we do know however is that the process is on auto-pilot from hereon in unless we can solve whatever caused the shift."

"You mean we're not in control, we didn't control it?" she asked with a frown. "I thought we always had "failsafe"?"

He shook his head. "Our "friends" lied. They are following some sort of pre-programmed routine. Trouble is they have been re-activated three light years too soon. We have come to the conclusion that they are of a "class" of worker on a par with maintenance crews and garbage details, they have no executive powers at all."

"Are you certain they aren't all the same? Have you tried any of the others?" she asked.

Jasmine had been sworn to secrecy when Rick had revealed to her the breathtaking discovery made on one of his earliest visits to the Moon. He had convinced her of the need for her absolute allegiance to him as a global responsibility with dire consequences should such information reach the wrong hands. Such was the strength of her belief in him that without a single protest her silence was guaranteed.

Rick had always been an adventurer, a maverick and something of a rebel on the early expeditions to the closest neighbour to Earth, the Moon. Because he bankrolled most of the expeditions, he was particularly fortunate in that he could control the game totally. It meant he had free access to Lunar travel whenever he wanted it too.

Despite his lack of engineering knowledge, his determination to be a part of its exploration was fuelled with the desire to control the vast potential in whatever way he could. His head was filled with images of early space exploration, of shuttle flights and the famous Apollo landings with all of their enigmatic codes and messages. He had always thought that there was more to this particular satellite than early NASA missions had let on. That plus his knack for being in the right place at the right time, and an intuition beyond measure were again proven right within just a few flights.

Quite by chance on one of his many solitary explorations of remote regions around the orb, driven by some chance recordings of one of the Apollo missions recon flights low over the surface which hinted at irregular magnetic readings, his fantasies became the reality. Well clear of the regular and predetermined excavations, and those he called the "Moon Rapers", he chanced upon a particular formation which in contrast to the irregular layout of the beautiful unspoilt lunarscape around him, marched as far as the eye could see in a perfectly straight line north to south. The particular depression he was in seemed to be sheltered from the rest of the terrain to the extent that the normally thick layer of moon dust wasn't in evidence. Patches of bare rock punctuated the shallow between the ravine walls. As he drove the buggy into the bottom of the ravine his initial impression was reinforced as the sunlight reflected from the surface and the clear outline of a rift showed through. As he drove the buggy over the fissure, its weight broke the fragile crust almost catapulting him from the vehicle. Once he had established the extent of the damage, and was satisfied running repairs would get him back to base safely, he made a further exploration of the hole he had made. When he had made the hole large enough to enter, he found a structure that was neither man-made nor a natural phenomena.

It took many return trips, all in total secrecy, before he penetrated beyond the outer walls. It then took a sizeable amount of resource and his most devious scheming to bring the most brilliant minds he could buy to work on the project, not to mention a considerable amount of money. Whilst raising the necessary capital had not been too difficult, justifying the expenditure to an astute "sniffer dog" like Old Tom had proven irritatingly harder. Tom fortunately was an insatiable academic at heart, and was somewhat mollified with the extra facilities subsequently put at his disposal. It was only in the more advanced stages of the exploration that Tom's interference proved an obstacle. His death was timely enough for all that it was regrettable, but Rick had managed to persuade himself that this was one particular end worth almost anything in the way of sacrifice - as long as he was in control.

Discovering the cryogenics chambers was awesome in itself. The next few years were frustratingly slow as the secrets behind the technology controlling them were gradually decoded, or so he had thought. Now he realised he had been duped! Whatever was happening now could easily wreck all of his carefully laid plans, unless he could wrest back the initiative somehow. Now that the first stages of the 'alien' plan had been apparently initiated by the aliens themselves and not according to the agreement he believed he had with them, Rick began to see his advantage slipping away.

His interrogation of the first of the creatures they had revived had revealed the presence of a machine of enormous power planted at the very core of this dead world many eons earlier. As to its ultimate use none of the subjects they had revived could or would elaborate, forcing Rick to concede that they were not dealing with the 'masters' of the "master race".

The appeal of great power always spurred him on, and the possibility of this potential for limitless power was an aphrodisiac he pursued with even more vigour than usual. The prospects of the untold wealth it might create were of no consequence to him, he was already a very wealthy man. But power, now that was quite another thing altogether. There lay the real satisfaction.

But now he had a different threat to contemplate. His was no longer the controlling hand, if not him, then who? If this device were really on alien "autopilot", he had no way of knowing what was on their agenda, and that worried him more than anything else. He would just have to find out what their motives were. If they could display such logic and intelligence, then they could be reasoned with and a deal struck at some point. The only question was the price. He turned back to face Jasmine.

"When the device was activated, this display schematic came on line at the same time that all the external activity took place." he indicated an array of screens glowing with a red 3D illustration of a sphere. "Look at this closely. Imagine an orange. Imagine the segments on one half of the fruit pulled out one by one in opposite directions. They have a shuttering effect revealing more and more of the surface beneath. The only purpose of this action must be to release the device that was planted here for an as yet unknown purpose. The side of the Moon pointing away from Earth now is the one where all the activity is taking place. What's to say that this same mechanisation won't swing the Moon around until the affected side faces Earth and then who knows what the consequences will be."

"Dad, why did you let Mike die?" she asked suddenly "You left him at the airlock to die. Why? He could have helped us, he's an astro-engineer. He could have been invaluable. I'm sure he would have done it for me if I'd asked him."

"He's alive and well" Rick replied. "Last I heard he's set about tracking you down. Right now he's somewhere in the maze of gangways and corridors heading for Central Hall. I may not like the guy; he's impetuous, quick tempered and reckless but he's not stupid. I would never harm him. I'll get my people to bring him in soon, just to please you. How about that?"

Jasmine didn't reply. He hoped she believed him, he hoped she was right about Mike. Besides, she just might be right, his knowledge could be useful to get them through this crisis. 'If I were Mike', he mused, 'surely I wouldn't want to risk losing her now, not Jas.'

CHAPTER SEVEN: WITHIN THE ROCK

Mike began to piece together the reason behind Jasmine's speedy departure. The chamber he was in appeared to be some kind of staging area with corridors leading away in a radial pattern all around the circumference. By walking all the way round he calculated that it measured about one mile across. None of the corridors distinguished itself from any of the others. In fact the only remarkable feature appeared to be the lack of dust or debris of any kind. Either someone or something was extremely meticulous in their housekeeping, or there was some kind of automated maintenance process at work here.

The source of lighting in the chamber was also puzzling him. Not overtly noticeable, there was a kind of subdued glow that emanated from the fabric of the walls themselves providing just enough illumination to see the entire space around him clearly.

Mike returned to his discarded gear and sat down. He tried to put himself in Jasmine's shoes and decide what she would have made of this development. What would she be thinking, what would she have done, which direction would she take, why hadn't she waited to see if he followed her through the airlock? If she had panicked with the closing of the outer door and gone on to penetrate the inner door, what then? Maybe she had begun to search for a way back, taken off her suit to allow for faster movement. Once inside, she had not found anything to guide her back to the surface and probably changed tack and begun to explore the chamber and its corridors. Whilst that made perfect sense to him in normal circumstances, these particular circumstances were anything but normal. This was a relic of alien origin and human logic was not guaranteed to prevail. Whilst they had successfully decoded the entry key, now they had no means of accessing the exit door, even if they could locate one! That left the anonymous corridors, the next obvious way to go. But which one would she have chosen and why?

There was another thought nagging away at him which just would not manifest itself. Where had he come across something like this before? It definitely reminded him of something but what. He was just about to abandon the thought when it struck him dead centre.

One time during one of their early vacation trips, they had taken Magnoway 74 out of town to a favourite area of unspoilt landscape, a wild spot they had explored many times since their first visit. They had read about the survival of a natural phenomena and decided to check it out for real instead of the virtual reality movies provided by the library. The phenomena was located in one of the few remaining forested areas of the globe, well off the beaten track. They took the 4th turnoff the Magnoway after leaving the city outskirts. The metalled surface petered out after 10 miles or so leaving them a trek of another 6 miles before they reached their goal. The forest eventually engulfed them completely, shutting out the blue sky and the remorseless sun above, leaving them in a new world of green light and cool shade in stark contrast to the white light and rugged terrain they'd left behind a mere 10 minutes earlier. When they stumbled across the sparkling waters of a broad stream, no words were needed as they each spontaneously discarded their clothing and dove into the clear blue waters laughing and splashing like children. They spent a few languid hours at the stream alternatively diving and swimming around each other alternating with periods of making leisurely love in the warm waters of a shallow rock pool.

Once sated and recovered, they continued their exploration of the wonders of this new experience, going further into the welcoming embrace of their new "wonderland". From their earliest years, they had been raised within the confines of the stone and marble environment of the city and had seldom ventured beyond the city boundaries with their parents, and had never before realised the treasure that was classed as the "wildlands" could possibly be such a pleasure. True there were still the die-hard naturists who petitioned long and hard for government funding to educate the population to make use of their natural environment. Mostly they were regarded as cranks and dreamers longing for the regressiveness of earlier times, a return to the "philosophy" of nature. Both Mike and Jasmine at that moment had become the most ardent of converts. However they had no intention of preaching to their fellow man, preferring to keep their newfound experience for themselves.

As they explored one particular tract of forest they came upon the fabled "maze" they'd read about in a pamphlet they had been given by one local "fanatic". The amazing sight of this natural formation left them spellbound and open-mouthed. They cautiously approached the only opening they could see. The "maze" had been formed by the intertwining of the trunks of many trees over a long period of time all striving to reach the light above, they had somehow woven an almost impenetrable wall of living foliage. As they stood in the clearing at the entrance and looked about them, they got the impression that they were standing at the axis of a huge wheel, the "spokes" formed by the green lit tunnels radiating away in all directions, left and right as well as forwards, and of course one of which was the way they had just come. The temptation to explore these inviting green openings with the speckled light of the sunlight above creating an ever-changing lighting display effect was irresistible. The whispering of the breeze as it gently rustled and sang through the complex added a magical backdrop to their whole experience.

Before setting out to explore their new world, they took the precaution of tying off the end of a plassam streamer. This was an ever-stretchable multi-coloured fabric which no matter how hard it was pulled or how long it was stretched always recoiled into its retaining pouch. No self respecting scout cadet ever left home without his ball of plassam! They had tossed the old accessory into their kit bag more as a joke than anything, mocking Mike's father who would religiously remind him to take it on every trip with the scouts as a boy with the motto "Stand ready, stand safe!" as his parting words.

With a jerk, Mike returned to the present with the realisation that all the daydreaming in the world would not find her. What he had concluded was that if she had left no trail behind her, she must have been forced to leave under protest, against her will. In a way that idea pleased him, she hadn't just abandoned him after all. A quick check through her equipment revealed the plassam pouch. Now all that remained was for him to track down her abductors and then worry about getting both of them safely back to base.

He anchored the loose end of the streamer with a matter-tack having chosen to enter the corridor directly opposite the entrance to the cavern. If they had taken her inward, then there must eventually be some kind of staging post or base buried deep beneath the lunar surface, so logically, at 90 degrees to his entry point, he was heading toward the satellite's core.

He estimated that he had travelled about 2 kilometres when he found himself at the first of many corridor intersections. There were at least 8 new options for him to consider at this point with diagonal as well as vertical and horizontal cross-overs.

"Always move to your left" Jasmine had boldly declared as they entered the forest maze through the first inviting passage they encountered. "That way at least if we do get lost, we're bound to pick up our own trail sooner or later."

Several hours later and many miles travelled, some on hands and knees others at a comfortable height, they emerged from the maze, but only after they had retraced their steps following the simple trail they had left.

"Right it is then!" said Mike to the junction emphatically with a smile. He took just 100 steps into the new corridor and froze in his tracks.

Jasmine could not sleep. She felt guilty. Guilty at having abandoned Mike and guilty about all the lies and deception. Restless in thought, she began to question her own motives even the very reason she was here on the Moon at all.

She recalled the many times her father had expressed his concerns and warnings for her. How he had told her of his fears of the many death threats on both his and her lives, about the many thwarted attempts to remove him from his position as head executive of the most powerful corporation in the world. He had produced compelling evidence which suggested that even his partner and life-long friend, in his quest for wider recognition and acclaim for his discoveries was not to be considered above suspicion. He even revealed to her plots discovered on secret micro-vids showing Tom and Mike in earnest and secretive discussions behind closed doors. That was never Tom's usual way of doing things.

She also recalled her feelings of horror and abject despair at being torn between the two of them; between the man she adored and the man she loved. She could scarcely believe that Mike would ever keep, would ever want to keep secrets from her. She thought she had known everything there was to know about him and yet here was the proof of that before her own eyes. Suspicion gave way to anger and in turn frustration whenever she would raise the topic of his self imposed isolation, he refused to even acknowledge the question. She knew within herself that she was as much responsible for the inevitable moods and attitude problems which dominated their home life as he was. She also knew that in the end, it had been her coldness and rejections which had severed their intimate bond irrevocably and drove Mike away in despair and self-pity. She believed and trusted only one other man more than her lover and turned towards him for support and comfort. She was barely surprised when Mike packed his things and moved out of their treasured apartment to begin his life again as he heeded the beckoning call for skilled engineers on this very Lunar project. She saw less and less of him as he spent long periods up there. She even sensed the changes in herself as she adapted to Rick's ways, suspecting and mistrusting anybody outside of the coveted inner circle. Though she hated herself for changing this way, it became her shield, her armour. Behind it she stood unchallenged and invincible, aloof and alone. She learned to live for herself alone. She became ambitious and ruthless, tolerating nothing but perfection. Even the tragic death of Mike's father failed to penetrate the fortress. Where she should have been a comfort to him, she ignored Mike completely, abandoning him to his pain and misery.

To add to his troubles, the last vestiges of his involvement in the company were officially removed. The only interest she could show was disdain for the lack of fight he had put up. He had simply walked away.

And yet now, here in this crazy situation, they had found each other again. Of all people he had been the one to have "rescued "her. She couldn't help but admit that the rekindling of the flame had affected her deeply and her feelings for him were growing stronger all the time. She also began to feel an uncomfortable feeling too, one that she wasn't at all sure about, and one that she could not guarantee to keep under control. These feelings were beginning to get in the way of her mission. She realised that she was concerned for him and about him at the same time. She knew he would be searching for her now. Her sudden disappearance defied logic, he would assume the worst and come after her. She knew him well enough to know that if anything Mike was probably more dangerous when under pressure than at any other time. In his hands, desperation was a weapon not to be trifled with. She couldn't work out why, but she suddenly recalled their trip to the "wildlands" in the national park, and their encounter within the natural phenomena known as the "Maze". As they were exploring the tunnels created by the intertwining of the forest, they had had the misfortune to disturb one of the few remaining wildcats that still lived in the wilderness. Their exit from one of many small chambers was cut off by the 'cat as it stalked them, angry at their intrusion into its domain. His first concern had been for her protection as he had pushed her behind him to face the cat himself. He tried to distract and deter the animal by hissing at it and baring his teeth whilst trying to circle and manoeuvre them around it. The strategy almost worked as they made it to the entrance of the lair before the Puma made its move leaping at them with claws flailing jaws wide open. With perfect timing, Mike had swung a vicious right hook which connected with such force that the cat simply dropped unconscious at their feet. They scrambled away to safety as fast as they could, picked up the plassam trail and back-tracked out of the "Maze" back to their base camp. Trembling with fear, her eyes shone with the excitement of their adventure, and she was secretly thrilled with her hero. She believed then that nothing could ever separate them. Sadly that was proven to be untrue.

She remained only half convinced by her father's assurances for his safety, but even less convinced of the adverse effect Mike could have on the entire project. On this issue she did not believe that they had done enough to prevent him from causing them trouble and inconvenience at this advanced stage. If anyone anywhere posed a potential threat to their activities it would have to be him of all people. She was also torn, deeply troubled and unhappy to be regarding him as a "hostile" when her heart was telling her otherwise.

Before laying down to sleep, she whispered a private prayer for his safety. Her sleep was troubled and dark.

CHAPTER EIGHT: JACK'S RETURN

The nearer he got to the surface the more surreal was the picture unfolding below him. He knew what he was looking at but it didn't register as any place he'd been before. Jack looked above and to each side of the work pod. He was in the company of several large slivers of moon debris, ever moving and ever threatening to engulf and smash the frail craft as it gingerly groped its way back to the relative safety of the lunar surface. Any one of these monsters could easily crack the fragile outer shell of his ship. As a precaution he donned a pressure suit and concentrated on threading his way downward through the rising obstacle course below him. As he looked down at the new moon surface he thought how bizarre it now appeared; one section smooth and metallic contrasting starkly with the usual pock marked white brilliance on either side reflecting the harsh rays of the sun. He imagined a metal sphere beneath the cover of dust, a thought that did little to calm his nerves.

Once in clear space and free of the dangers of loose rocks, he ran a fresh diagnostic on his instruments; not good! The effort of tearing himself free of the wedge had depleted his energy reserves well beyond the safety margins. It was touch and go whether he would have sufficient power for a controlled descent let alone return to the moon base over 1000 kilometres away. His oxygen reserves were nearing empty and to top it all off, he had lost communications. His antennae had been ripped off in the final scraping manoeuvre that launched him clear of the slab. Of his 10 thruster packs only 6 were operational, and two of those were intermittent at best. No he was definitely not in good shape!

'Ah well' he sighed 'it could be worse. At least I'm OK for wate....' His voice trailed off as he watched the water reserve canister detach itself and float away, yet more evidence if it were needed that the craft had taken one hell of a pounding. He was lucky to be alive and he knew it, thanks to Mike.

Jack thought hard before making up his mind. He decided he had one chance and only one chance to survive. He kicked in the power and pointed the nose towards Mike's last known position and what he hoped would be safety. He was relieved when the homing signal of Mike's pod chimed in. Of the 'Streak' there was no sign. Hopefully the autopilot had done its job and returned the mother ship back to base. He locked on to the signal and trusted the failing systems of his own craft to last out until lunarfall, and to guide him to his new objective. As soon as he relinquished control he began to stuff every compartment of his suit with anything he thought would be useful for survival.

The closer he got to his objective, the less easy he felt. The primitive autopilot was coping well enough at least!. Within 15 minutes of executing the flight plan, he found himself within striking distance of their original co-ordinates, and was relieved when he finally set eyes upon Mike's ship. It was still perched where Mike and Jasmine had left it as described, on the lip of the "portal" they had mentioned in their last transmission. Jack just stared in fascination at the metalled walls and wondered as they had done as to its origins and purpose. He could see no sign of them, nor could he raise them on either their personal communicators or on the ship to ship channel.

He made what was for him a better than average touch down, especially under these circumstances and the decidedly unstable condition of his ship. He secured the shut down and exited his ship, and went over to Mike's. A quick check revealed everything in order and on stand by. Wherever they had gone, they were obviously planning to return. The Quorum team bank containment tank was standing near the hatch so he took it with him in the hope that they could help him repair his pod. It was then he noticed a device of some kind, a recorder, facing the blank wall within the flange area. On closer examination he recognised its purpose. It was scanning a light sequence emanating from the wall. An unlocking mechanism device maybe? He climbed down from the ship and walked over to the wall. The recorder was no longer active. Presumably it had done its work and gained them entry to whatever was behind this rock/ metal wall. He regarded it as odd that they had not left any indication of their intentions on the ship's log. That would be normal protocol. He reasoned that in these circumstances, their entry must have been made under extraordinary circumstances.

As he considered his next move, he recognised what was becoming a regular event lately. A low vibration followed by a rising level of audible rumbling and dust clouds. This time though he heard something else. Turning to face the gaping chasm he understood the nature of this new sound. The opposite side of the rift was closing in on his side fast, too fast for an escape via the pods he realised with a start.

If he didn't act soon he would be sandwiched within the flange as its opposite number bore down on him. He backed away instinctively as he faced up to the inevitable. Looking round he glanced again at the sequence of lights in the wall. If this was a lock where was the key? He powered up the recorder, more an act of desperation than anything and on a whim activated the replay mode. Nothing happened! He backed away again, grim faced, as the gap between the two sides of the Kanyan were close enough to be shutting out the light. It would soon be crushing the ships and then he was next. As he backed away again he reached the face of the wall, but instead of solid rock behind his back, he fell through! Picking himself up he registered his position and realised the wall was an elaborate air lock. Thinking fast he also realised it was an air lock that was about to be breached by the remains of two crushed space vehicles. If and when that happened the inner door to the airlock would be sealed with him on the wrong side of the door for sure. Running as fast as his pressure suit allowed, he ran the length of a short curved corridor, relieved to find the inner door of the airlock at the end. Without hesitation he hit the wall at full stretch. As he went through, something caught his left leg and he fell to the ground. Looking back he could see that the material of the door had begun to solidify and had him by the ankle of his boot. Without thinking he shed his suit and dropped to the floor in relief at his escape. Only then did he realise his stupidity! Yet he was breathing oxygen! As he began to rise, he stopped in his tracks at the sight of six pairs of black shiny boots standing in a circle around him. Hauled unceremoniously to his feet, black uniforms devoid of any insignia or markings topped off with anonymous black visors, this was the last thing he remembered before he felt a sharp sting in his arm, a bright starburst of light in his head and then a black nothingness.

CHAPTER NINE: EXODUS

Dhoran checked over the readings yet again. The delicate balance factors were a very fine judgement to call at this crucial time and if he was to succeed he could not afford a displacement factor of more than 0.3%. He grunted in satisfaction at the display readout of 0.25%. 'Of all the times for this to be happening' he thought complaining inwardly. Their survival, their very existence could very well depend on these next few moments and his skills.

"Dhoran! We must go! Now!" His Second-In-Command stood hovering uncertainly at the entrance. "The last few ships are loading and departing as soon as they are secure. There remain but three at the dock. We will be left behind! Please!"

"Go Korin! You must go with them. There is still so much to do here, I cannot leave until I am satisfied it is complete. I have my drones to support me, your family needs you. Go now! That is my order. Go now!"

That had confirmed it. Dhoran turned back to his calculations and fine-tuning of the instrument panel. This was to be his moment. Never before in the entire history of his race had the opportunity presented itself to one individual to perform such an unbelievable feat of engineering and ingenuity in the service of its continuity. The culmination of his life's work would have ensured its survival if only they had listened to him before it had passed beyond the point of no return. Now all he could do was to bring the doomed project to a conclusion in the vain hope that all would not be wasted. Where he had aspired to adulation he could but enjoy pity and recognition, perhaps due gratitude. But now by this decision he had forfeited even this crumb of self-congratulation and comfort. To retain his own sanity he focused his thoughts on the high points in his life; his two loved and lost wives his families and this last and enduring monument to his labours. How short-sighted, how cowardly of his people, how uninspired was his fellow man in the jaws of catastrophe that they could only flee, when he had provided their deliverance. They did not believe him; they could not see the moment of glory. For too long they had resisted the inevitable and deprived his project of the most vital of components, money, at the time when it was most needed. Now it was too late. They had gambled and lost. But there was still a chance for him. He knew how it would be, he knew he would survive. The question now was had he done enough in time?

Their world had seen more than its fair share of conflict, greed, power struggles and political mayhem. There had been a realisation of their wildest dreams when the golden era of civilisation dawned in the 3rd millennium of their history. Global unification had been surprisingly easy to achieve once the ugliness of their mass of weapons of self destruction had been put aside for ever and the spectre of fear banished as a result. Global integrity and global re-unification's proliferated at every strata of society. Dhoran smiled inwardly as he recalled his own inner relief at the mass rejection of the greatest of all Mankinds' folly. The nightmare days were banished forever. In their place great strides had taken over both the physical and spiritual needs of the people and generated a new purpose for all. No more would they suffer the seemingly unstoppable decline in their moral and social standards. And the catalyst of this enlightenment? That had come from the skies above too. The destruction of the continent of Antilec by a random meteor hit had galvanised the finest scientific brains into a collective fever of discovery and co-operation to provide a solution for practically every known threat to their world.

He recalled the event itself very clearly as happening in his first lifespan when as a youngling barely out of school the skies had become permanently dark and forbidding. The resultant crop failures and storms resulted in famine around the world

Claiming a great many lives, including those of his own parents in only their 3rd lifespan. He felt even now a pang of sorrow that they were not here to witness his greatest triumph, and to see the way in which their world had progressed to this higher level of tolerance and understanding. That catastrophe had probably everything to do with his chosen path of study. From student to teacher to professor, from politician to scientist and ultimately his worlds best known and most respected theologian.

The golden age following the event was marked with genuine desire for a sharing of all knowledge, technology, resource, wealth and purpose resulting in the forerunner to modern society today. The wearisome tedium of everyday life was eliminated entirely with the application that the new technologies made possible. Hunger, disease, social imbalance inequality; each were tackled in turn and eliminated. The need for work for personal gain no longer existed. People worked for the good of others. Crime was gone completely, its causes all eliminated in turn. Pollution and the environment were the primary motivation of everybody's lives for decades until the ecological dream became a wonderfully liberating reality. A modern paradise once long forgotten was rescued and enjoyed as it was originally intended.

An idyllic age enjoyed by the entire population. Until of course his grim discovery that there existed an even worse nightmare than they had been able to imagine to this point, a nightmare which threatened their Utopian existence. With the freedom to explore anything and everything, Dhoran had continued to study the stars and the heavens, giving all his energies and knowledge to the expanding of their knowledge of the world and the universe at large. During one of his inspired projects of discovery, he had encountered this new nightmare for the first time. Deep space scanners had identified a threat to their world; one which dwarfed the Antilec incident into insignificance by comparison. Only when he had exhausted every possible outcome but the ultimate destruction of their very existence on the planet did he dare make his discovery public knowledge. The validity of his discovery was undisputed, but the determination of their response to the threat was not that straightforward. With a high degree of accuracy, this new threat was determined to be at least 100 years in the future, that they could predict with reasonable accuracy and all agree upon. Exactly what to do about the threat was less clear. There were of course sceptics who argued that the degree of significance was wide enough to allow for a near miss with the planet, and therefore urged no action at all. At the other extreme were the prophets of doom that basked in the self inflicted satisfaction of impending disaster as the retribution for the idyllic life of the entire planet. The world government however recognised the potential of the disaster to be and began making plans to eliminate the threat, taking

Dhoran's suggestions as the centrepiece of their strategy. Until that is they discovered the New World, at the furthest extremity of their sensor capability on the very edge of the known universe, during the 75th year after the discovery of the threat from space. Up to that point Dhoran had devised a project which all agreed to be the ultimate solution to their vulnerability. All had agreed to support him and to provide the resource and finance to make his vision a reality. With a new option and solution available to them however, the once solid support for the original solution began to waver. Fuelled by petty arguments and jealousies, long since forgotten emotions within the "new way", doubt upon doubt was heaped upon Doran's "folly" as some were beginning to refer to the project. A faction in the Government who held great power and influence with the incumbent President proposed another option of exodus from Earth. In fairness the President had engaged a great deal of debate and discussion before endorsing this second lifeline to mankind. It was therefore decided to continue with Dhoran's original plan but at a reduced pace, whilst endorsing the escape plan. This would involve the construction of multitudinous sites all over the globe for the construction and preparation of stellar ships to evacuate the entire population of the planet to the newly discovered world. It did seem as though providence had arrived in the nick of time to provide the ultimate solution. A New World of apparently as far as their limited scientific probes and telescopes could tell, roughly the same size, composition and nature of Earth, apparently uninhabited, and seemed to literally offer a heaven sent opportunity. Support and demand for this solution grew steadily with each passing year until the emphasis switched under the relentless pressure from defensive response to the threat to an active one. Consequently Dhoran found himself practically begging for the materials and resource to complete his project. It seemed like only he had an unshakeable belief in the ability to defend their world against the seemingly unstoppable force heading their way. Exodus was the popular choice and support for the movement began to increase the nearer the threat came.

Now as he put the final pieces into place, Dhoran reflected upon his inability to convince the people with only his conviction and faith in this solution. Perhaps he too, if he was honest, had at some point doubted his ability to complete the project on time, or that his calculations on meeting the threat were correct in their assumptions. Whatever the reasons he knew in his heart that deserting the planet was not necessary, yet he understood the desire for exodus by everyone else as the inevitable consequence of giving people a choice. He alone knew that in diverting the resource into creating developing and building the stellar ships in the numbers needed, his own needs had at times been ignored. No one was to be left behind. No one but Dhoran that was!

Working completely alone now, as the remaining ships departed, he painstakingly completed the final stages of the finest feat of engineering ever undertaken by the human race, unobserved, unseen and unappreciated. He paused briefly to witness the last ship's launch with its precious human cargo. Now that the final link was gone, he determined to focus on the final touches. With hours counting down on the master board he wondered whether anybody would know how hard he had worked to avoid this catastrophe. The red section of the dial was activated and he realised with a sinking heart that he had failed at the end. There was no more time left. If the project was to have become effective, it should have been activated by now. Too late! He thought long and hard now and decided to fulfil his own ambition at least. After the last piece was installed and the simulation checked out as normal, he was satisfied that the project was complete and functional. He relieved his drone crew of their duties and returned them to their holding stations. With a reluctant hand, he began to close down each sector in turn until all activity on the board showed as de-activated. Finally he entered his own personal chamber and activated the device.

One hour after shut down, the planet bore the full force of the unprecedented anomaly obliterating all evidence of mans presence along with all of its vegetation, animals and boiling off all of its oceans. It took just 1 second.

CHAPTER TEN: EARTH RESPONSE

After the initial disbelief and terror towards the unfolding drama in the skies above, Earth's population fell back into the all too familiar routine of apathy and disinterest. For all of their fondness for the Moon, once it was apparent that their daily lives and routines were not affected, there seemed to be a resigned acceptance that the new profile presented to them was in fact just as it should be. Naturally there had been a huge outcry of disgust against the Government for the loss of so many lives. Demands for enquiries and safety standards reviews headlined the news for weeks on end whilst the haunting spectacle of so many ceremonies of remembrance and mourning filled the global networks. But once this passed, normality quickly returned in all quarters. Few if any faces were lifted in awe and wonder at the unfolding saga above their heads any more.

The leaders of the Quadrants, mindful of their ratings of popularity duly attended all the necessary congregations in their sorrow, sympathising publicly with the bereaved in sickening displays of false but necessary sentiment. As one they rose and spoke of reforms and tighter controls on the corporations, those faceless and non-accountable bodies, at whose doors they skilfully laid the blame.

Behind the façade however there lurked the growing concern of each one of the governing bodies. In the absence of any other data to the contrary, the visible changes on the Moon's surface proved only to fuel speculation as to the ultimate consequences of this unprecedented event. What was the purpose of this now newly recognised artificial satellite, Earth's faithful and up until this point docile companion? What further hazards would be revealed? Who had orchestrated this awesome sight and perhaps the most compelling and demanding question of all – why? The whisperers held that it could be a weapon of mass destruction, or that it could be a sign of some impending disaster. Still others held the view that it was a hoax, a diversion thought up by who-knows-who to soften the populace up against an imminent proclamation of one sort or another. The truth was that nobody knew for sure what was happening. Nobody had any reference point to guide them to a logical explanation. So they avoided the issue as much as they could by ignoring its presence and carrying on as before. By the time they had mobilised the necessary expeditionary forces and equipped and launched it, a further three weeks were lost.

By now, four weeks after the disaster, the only people in a position to shed any light on the situation were those already in situ on the Moon. Even so disaster seemed to dog every move they made. The three teams initially sent out to investigate the so-called "Grand Kanyan" had apparently disappeared without trace and it seemed as though the Moon itself was determined to shake off the rest of its snowy white mantle. Day after day more sections of the lunar surface were cast off revealing more and more of the dark metalled surface beneath.

Orson Cavel, Global President, was a natural born leader. A youthful 48, he commanded the respect of the entire senate irrespective of political persuasion or preference. With his amiable easy going style and his down to earth approachable nature, he portrayed the kind of man you wanted at your side whenever there was trouble. His handsome features and athletic build endeared him to the female population of voters reinforced by his natural charm and wit. Though his political rivals wished it otherwise, he lived a genuine family life, one in which he took great pleasure as well as pride. It was this strong foundation and his erstwhile conviction of true values, which singled him out as a man of honour and trust. Giving no favour of any kind, his genuine interest in the well being and welfare of his fellow man shone with a passion through his gentle brown eyes.

Not for nothing did his adversaries approach a face to face meeting with this man with some trepidation. Above all else he had the kind of courage of self-belief to persuade the most opposed view that whatever the circumstances might be, that right would always prevail, and he was usually right. Even so he was under no illusion that all the friendliness that he could muster would win every argument. His principles were dear to him, and homespun though they might be, he made sure that most people could identify with his objectives without his being condescending in any way.

It took a great deal to worry this man, and now he was deeply troubled. Something about the scale of the unfolding Moon drama told him that there must be an ultimate purpose or reason. The idea of a terrorist incursion, dreamed up by his vast army of advisors was not in his opinion to be easily tossed aside as soon as it had been aired. Implausible as it was facing the sheer scales of this enigmatic puzzle, he knew that some of the larger corporations with some of the latest advances could in theory consider tackling something on this scale. It was the motivation for doing so that held him in check, he knew most of the corporation chiefs personally and thought he knew their commitment to mans' aspirations as well as his own. For many years now the harmony between society and corporate needs had enriched all of society. There still existed of course those who believed in the advantages of free trade, prosperity, and self-improvement for gain, free enterprise and commerce. Such "revolutionaries" as existed were in the main small voices in the hubbub of this thriving and, for the most part contented population. Their activities railed against the so-called "nursery" society who considered today's society to be bland uninspired and unexciting. But they were certainly ineffective and small in comparison to this event. As time went by, now a month or so after the initial shock and discovery, there had been no demands, no insurrection, no indication that the threat came from Earth factions at all.

As he walked the familiar route to the debating chambers, he knew that he would be expected to provide the answer to the enigma, some sort of rationalisation or theory at the very least. He smiled in greeting as the CentraNet opened up to the waiting audience of countless billions of citizens. By far the most efficient and expedient means of communication with the seemingly ever-shrinking world population ever built, it was an immensely powerful governing tool. This session involved only the Quadrant Governors. Essential business was dealt with swiftly so that the key issue could enjoy full exposure and debate. 'This is not going to be an easy ride' he thought to himself as he addressed the 90 members of the Inner Council.

"WorldPeople, Greetings!" he began his address in the usual way in a display of controlled patience and confidence, as much for his own benefit as that of his audience. Without the merest hint of concern, the Earth president deftly handled the routine matters of Government with skill and astute dexterity, eliminating the myriad concerns and requests from the many regions and quadrants of the Earth. After he had spoken for two hours, he had successfully answered or deferred all of the questions placed at the dais for his consideration.

"We must now turn our attentions to the all too apparent issue of our neighbouring Moon and the changes seen to be taking place as we speak. Yes as we speak, we are monitoring and recording a metamorphosis as yet incomplete, and whilst we do not know the nature or the origins of the changes we see, we should consider all and every possible explanation together with an appropriate response. This will not be easy in the face of the extraordinary uncertainties and as yet unanswered questions but for sure, to do nothing at all is unacceptable. I ask you to listen now to Vice Counsel Drake with his analysis of the most recent developments and changes."

Chief Technologist and Vice Counsel to the Government, Victor Drake was the most eminent of the scientists of his day, and a specialist in Space Engineering. He faced the anxious attention of his global spectators somewhat bothered and bemused in the fashion of most science teachers as they faced questing minds in search of knowledge. Even though he had been thoroughly briefed by David Colton, Director of Lunar operations, he still felt as though there was more to the enigma that he should understand before facing these people.

"Our latest findings based on recent seismologic readings have indicated a mass of substrata activity suggesting the presence of forces beneath the Moon's surface. These forces have all the characteristics you might expect to see from the operation of massive plant or machinery underground

- like the old mining activity of two or three centuries ago here on Earth. The origins of such "machinery" are as yet unexplained, however they do not originate from here." Victor let that point sink in before continuing his presentation.

"As you will observe from the last image secured a few minutes ago, the result of the sub-lunar activity has produced some startling new revelations"

Like a half-finished school science project, the now familiar and ugly image of the far side of the formerly serene and friendly satellite appeared in front of the dais. The holographic image lit the chamber with a white reflected glow. With the missing segment of its surface, the resultant gap shown in full detail offered a sinister and evil aspect to the desolate and beautiful globe.

"There have been two further developments to report, each significant in themselves, but together they suggest a greater intelligence behind them than we had originally thought. Our current examination of these chang......"

Victor's voice faltered as the image in front of him firstly wavered and then blinked out altogether. In its place, seeming to stare right at him with unseen eyes behind a smooth black visor was the image of a man-like creature. The audio faders boomed into life as a message, which felt as though it originated from behind the beings' visor echoed around the chamber. The communication lasted only 15 seconds, too short and totally alien to the auto-translator system, and then ended with a click. The hologram re-appeared.

Orson leaned across to his Chief Aide. "Karl, I want you to get on that immediately. Find out why we couldn't decipher it, pinpoint the transmission point and get me the answers before Victor's finished. Ask the Director of the Quorum Corporation's crack team leaders to drop all other projects if necessary, we need answers and we need then right now! Oh and see if there is any link with that other garbled transmission report we picked up right after the first 'quake!" Karl Evan nodded his understanding and inconspicuously left the chamber to brief his team outside the doors before heading for his own office and data banks.

Orson stood up and motioned to the agitated gathering for silence to be heard.

"Members of the Counsel, we have all heard and seen yet another development in this mystery. Our research teams will be analysing the transmission whilst we continue the presentation, Dr Drake?"

"Thank you Mr President. As I was saying before our rude delegation interruption, the sub-strata activity, whilst it has displaced and ejected large areas of the lunar crust, also appears to have altered the chemical composition and substance of the geology. To what extent and by what means we must still determine. However externally, the end result of the appearance of the fissures, as you can see from the model, is followed by the expulsion of a segment of the surface which incredibly extends from pole to pole. Each segment measures 1 km across at its widest point. Currently there have been 200 such fissures on either side of the original manifestation, creating a gap of 400 kms. They occur at intervals of 5 minutes. We cannot explain the purpose of this exposure as yet. We have also detected a small but significant change in the nature of the Moon's status in orbit around us. The Moon has begun to rotate on its axis, albeit a small movement of ½ degree in the last twenty-four hours.

We think this is probably linked to the displacement of the surface material. If it continues to shed its' surface at the calculated rate, a segment of surface of 180 degrees will be completely removed in less than 10 days from now, and this far side will then be facing Earth. Again we do not know the reason behind this. For now our teams of engineers on the Moon itself and the research teams here are looking for any clues or explanations around the clock."

Karl, tapped the President on the shoulder and whispered his reported findings to him. Karl had discovered the origins to the transmission were a long since defunct derivative of the old binary system. His Quorum team had been hastily briefed to enhance, condense and translate the message into a recognisable format for the President. Its origin had been traced as having been relayed to Earth via the Moon from a point so far out on the unexplored and unknown edges of the galaxy that they had no point of reference for it. His best advice was that the message had been deliberately masked and encoded.

"In other words, we're none the wiser?"

"For the time being Mr President, yes" admitted Karl. "I'm sorry, we're doing everything we know how to track it down, but our satellite system is still in tatters and unlikely to improve in the short term. That and the ongoing lunar activity are screwing our probes up ....."

"OK Karl, I get the picture, don't take it personally." Orson smiled but was still frustrated by the news.

Questions and demands for further clarification were beginning to mount and grow to a noisy crescendo as Orson stood again to speak. This time the noise abated in one swoop of silence.

"Citizens, as you have heard for yourselves, events are overwhelming us as this session sits. Our scientists are working on the most recent transmission as we discuss this latest crisis. I call recess for three hours. I also order the final withdrawal of all but the most essential personnel from the stricken Moon project. They will meet our task force in space to better brief them on the situation. If there are further sigfnificant developments we need to brief you on urgently before resuming our session, we will reconvene in an emergency sitting. . Bon Chance!"

With the Summit in recess, Orson gathered his team of advisers, strategists and heads of Military together in closed session. Mark Turner and Andrea Markus, both tactical Commanders joined Karl and Victor. Andrea was Chief of Staff, and Mark specialised in Space Commando. After a short pause for refreshments Orson called the meeting to order.

"Karl, could you please fill us all in on your findings?" invited President Orson.

"Yes Sir. I can report some significant progress since our last meeting with the content of the latest message. The structure of the language used is a complex matrix configuration of the binary structure extended by a four sided dimension extract resulting in compression ratio of one : one thousandth."

"In plain language please?"

"Sir the original message was of 10 seconds duration. The actual message is 10 minutes in length, and can now be translated into any language we choose. The key was in the final "click" we heard. We can run it through the Global translators."

"Do we have a translation yet?"

"Yes Sir, I'll run it through now." said Karl nervously.

"It is still a little fragmented, the quality of the transmission is flawed, but there is sufficient body to get the gist."

" People of Earth. This is a message of warning of ………disaster about……strike you. Planet Earth is under atta……… severe repercussions if you do not hee…… warning. Our ships are poise…….. . Evacuation is imperative! Any attempt ………..resistance…………dealt with severely!"

Karl paused the transmission. "It gets very garbled at this point Sir for most of the next phase. They transmit what looks like co-ordinates and positions and technical data for about 6 minutes or so. I'll skip to what we believe is the punch line."

"You are instructed to heed this warning. Prepare to evacuate Mother Earth forever. …….future existence depen…………………………………………….."

"That's as much as we got sir," said Karl. "The rest is just static and nonsense."

They all sat in stunned silence as they absorbed the sight, and now the sound, of the rude messenger until finally the President broke the spell.

"We are certain as to the authenticity of this? No don't answer that Karl, you're too thorough by half! So it seems ladies and gentlemen that we are at risk and in grave danger. From who or what is not fully clear, but we can be certain that these events we are witnessing are now linked to this threat. Do we all agree?"

"Excuse me Mr President," Amanda Markus stood at the head of the table. "As Chief of Staff I must remind you that my Office must confirm any hostile act before taking any further decision. As yet we cannot know from that transmission that they are hostile to us, there are just too many gaps. We need to know the entire message, what are the co-ordinates describing, where are they showing us? I need more than fragments."

"Agreed Ms Markus, but we can agree that this message together with the irregularities in the sky above give us reasonable cause to consider that the two events may be linked and therefore pose a threat to our security which cannot be ignored, yes? We may also consider that the placid satellite we think of as a benign and trusted friend may not be all it seems. A threat Ms Markus is a threat and I don't think we have too much time as it stands to prepare a suitable response. Make preparations for the worst case scenario and then we will consider the nuances of the evidence. Those are my instructions. We may even have to go so far as to eliminate the Moon itself to safeguard our survival. Prepare the simulation programmes for all eventualities, all eventualities Ms Markus.

Karl, take the transmission apart piece by piece. I want your guys to go through it with every enhancer and decoder at their disposal. Make sure they double check everything with Quorum. I want the entire message unfolded and translated before we move. Have something ready for me in two hours. Where's Mark Turner? Mark, I want you to begin tactical planning for an assault on the Moon base as an exercise. Drill your men in readiness. When you have a workable plan for the destruction of a body of that size, I want a full briefing with Amanda and all the Quadrant Commanders in the field. Victor get your people to work on the effects of such a situation, environmental implications and effects. Let's meet back here in 24 hours people; with answers!"

Orson watched in satisfaction as each of his key people set about their designated tasks. Only then did he allow himself the luxury to contemplate the enormity of the challenge and the threat before them. He did not dwell upon the possibility of failure. In his minds' eye saw only his wife and the children and absently smiled.

CHAPTER ELEVEN: EXPLORATION

Trapped! He just could not breathe. The walls seemed to have closed around him and he couldn't get through. It felt as though he was treading water but making no headway at all. Molten rock poured through a fissure burning the skin from his body. He screamed and woke from the nightmare with a jolt.

Having trudged on and on for what seemed like an eternity for in reality just 6 hours, he had come across a rare niche in the smooth surface of the wall of the seemingly endless corridors of rock. Exhausted and disheartened by the monotony of the journey, he had welcomed the excuse to stop and rested within the sparse shelter it offered him, from what he didn't really know, but at this point had been too weary to care as he shrugged off and discarded his survival kit.

Now as he broke out a fresh ration pack, he began to suppress the welling feeling of frustration at his apparent lack of progress. He knew he could not hope to know whether the direction he was travelling was leading anywhere, or indeed whether or not he was going round in circles for that matter. He knew for a fact that the corridor never ran straight for more than a hundred metres simply from his rudimentary instruments and line of sight reckoning.

During the course of his walk, he had had lots of time to consider his situation and the many possibilities afforded by his position. His prime concern was assimilating the extent of the technology behind his current surroundings. If the airlock he had experienced was any indication then he could very easily be standing right next to other similar devices of unknown function and be none the wiser as to how to access the secrets of this sub lunar world. Then how far should he continue to travel along the corridor? Should he be retracing his steps back to the airlock and his ship? Subconsciously, perhaps for comfort, he tugged on the end of the line of plassam tape.

On first entering the corridor, he had been pretty badly shaken up by an encounter with what he imagined to be a guard of some kind. It had turned out to be nothing more than an empty suit of a fashion and material he had never seen before. It was suspended from a peg high on the wall of a similar niche to the one he was sitting in now. The effect created the impression that it was occupied. 'Maybe that was the idea' he had thought to himself 'as a warning?' The black material presented a sinister, menacing image, especially the black visor on the facemask, which in his imagination was watching his approach and every move with a detached apathy. Only after he realised there had been no movement from his observer for a full and long two minutes had he ventured forward and discovered the suit was an empty shell. The hieroglyphics above and around the niche looked similar to the markings that he and Jasmine had observed at the airlock. Whoever or whatever had occupied the suit in height and build was very human-like much to Mike's relief. 'No green-eyed monsters then!' he thought.

Now refreshed after a full four-hour rest, and suitably fortified by his protein enriched field pack, he began to revise his plan for the next few hours. He was about to step out into the corridor for a further 4 hour trek when he paused and listened to an unusual but regular sound that appeared to be coming his way. He glanced quickly around the edge of the niche and saw an apparatus that seemed to be all flailing arms and spray. The multi-armed machine was barrelling along the corridor, filling it with its bulk from floor to ceiling, efficiently and automatically cleaning the area ahead and around it with almost noiseless ease. 'That explains the lack of dust and debris then' he mused. As the machine passed by his respite, first soaking and then drying him in one action, Mike realised his opportunity had arrived. If this thing had a base or destination, then he could save a lot of legwork and hitch a ride. Quickly gathering his kit, he timed his move into the corridor as the machine cleared the edge of the niche. With a smooth movement, he located a convenient handhold and pulled himself aboard pleased at himself and at the first sign of good fortune to come his way so far. Pretty soon the monotony of his lonely slog through the corridor on foot was replaced by the tedium of riding this oversized domestic cleaner. Broken only by changes in direction and incline, the machine lumbered on with its uninvited guest aboard. Mike was almost dosing when the terminal was eventually reached confirming his assumptions of a maintenance operation. Only the disappearance of the comforting sound of spraying water alerted him to his imminent arrival at journeys end. The arms retracted next, and as he looked over the top of the machine he saw the wall open as if on cue to allow the cleaner to enter the rock and the chamber beyond. Once the power was cut, and he was sure he was not being watched, Mike dropped off the machine and walked to its "front" just in time as the device reversed into a tailored shape in the rock face to his left.

Careful to avoid detection, he made his way slowly forward until he reached a small entrance to another chamber. For at least the third time since entering the airlock as he stood at the doorway, Mike froze at the scene beyond. He was watching 6 figures clad in the uniform black suits he had encountered at the start of the corridor. They appeared to be arguing amongst themselves in a language which, although familiar to his ear, was unlike any other language he knew of. That was not the most important consideration though. The object of their attention and obvious agitation was secured to the opposite wall. It was Jack!

After at least 30 minutes, apparently frustrated at the lack of response to their efforts to get a response from Jack, the black suits left the room together. Waiting only until he was certain that they were not coming back immediately, Mike entered the chamber and approached Jack's inert body. He got no response and assumed they had knocked him out during their animated interrogation. Nothing he tried could bring the youngster round. His eyes though open were unseeing. At least here, he was glad that the kid was relatively safe rather than exposed to the void of space. If Jack were here then maybe Jasmine would be too!

Satisfied that there was nothing more he could do for Jack, Mike placed a hastily written message in his unconscious hand. Instinctively it seemed Jack's fingers curled around the note. From his backpack, he took out the alien space-wear he had appropriated at his rest-stop, and quickly put it on. Lightweight and extremely flexible, it seemed to mould itself to his body. Naturally there was no way he could continue to haul his survival kit whilst in disguise. He stashed his gear behind one of the storage containers along with his own space suit and the bulk of his equipment. Rigging a makeshift belt as his only concession to personal security, he carried only the plassam, his personal log and his trusty stunner. Though his main defence was stealth and cunning, the sight of Jack's plight illustrated only too plainly how exposed and vulnerable he was. These were not friendly aliens at all!

He was grateful for the small things. At least the doors in the complex were of fairly conventional design, almost boringly functional in fact. He opened the door to the corridor beyond just a fraction at first and peeped through. The black visor was surprisingly clear from the inside, and incorporated visual monitors of some description showing up as gridlines and graph maps as he tilted his head, but not intrusively. With a little practise, he learned how he could activate their appearance and gained a degree of personal satisfaction from his small triumph of control. The corridor on the left of the door was clear, he could see that. To check the other side would mean he had to enter it, so it was one of those 'now or never' moments. Decisively he stepped out of the room. Unchallenged he turned to his right and almost immediately came across a large set of double doors. The symbols around these doors gave no clues to him as to what lay on the other side. Taking another deep breath they opened easily and noiselessly to his touch as he entered. Once inside, he understood the purpose of this particular chamber with a another dose of deja-vu thrown in for good measure. One of his areas of specialised study had included the preservation of human and animal life so he knew on sight the purpose of the cryogenic devices in front, above and below him. Standing on a gallery platform, he was staggered by the sheer scale of the operation. Every direction he looked, banks upon banks of chambers were stacked in relays of 20 in a block. Those nearest to him appeared to be unoccupied, Whether the others were active or not was questionable, as a light, blue mist pervaded the entire room, diffusing the little light that was emitted from the concealed source.

He was even more staggered after he had passed a further 5 sets of similar rooms and pondered yet again upon the complexities of this endlessly unfolding enigma. Then he struck lucky. A shaft of yellow light spilled across the corridor floor from a doorway to a room about 30 metres ahead. From the partially open door came the unmistakable clamour of an active computer station. So far Mike had not encountered a soul, grateful not to be challenged. Still on guard, he cautiously approached the door and looked around the frame. Inside he saw banks of computers tended by scores of technicians he guessed. This was a cause for a double take. This could be a normal sight on the Moon-base itself if it were not for the black uniform suits and black-visored personnel. The one thing he did not expect to encounter here was the presence of what could only be a Quorum team at work, their characteristic paleness and lack of substance the unmistakable hallmark of a bad maintenance programme. They were obviously oblivious to his presence. They were dressed, as he was, in the all covering black suit, 'At least I'll blend in' he thought to himself. He sat down at a vacant workstation and watched the various monitors with their symbols of flashing colour sequences; their messages totally lost on him. The schematics were a different story, those were his domain. Flexing and cracking his knuckles and fingers he became more and more immersed in the symbols as he tried to make sense of the alien drawings. They appeared to be directly linked to the developing structure of the moon he felt sure he could sense rather than interpret the connection, but he couldn't understand why. Some of the data he recognised as internal structural plans highlighting stress factors and points of potential weakness. Others appeared to be of a routine service function, passageways access points and route maps. The system was obviously scrolling at random through its memory banks, perhaps triggered by untrained hands. As he continued to watch, the schematics occasionally showed something that made sense. One aspect of a machine or devise suggested to him the way the final configuration of several previous flashes had been illustrating perhaps the devise that was forming on the surface? The other illustrations seemed to flow around this design, scale and co-ordinates seemed to fit, but the main question of its purpose was still elusive. Earth itself appeared briefly as a blue and white marbled ball in the right configuration and in the correct proportions as seen from the lunar surface. Looking around at his "companions", they all appeared to be having the same difficulty as he was. They did not seem to be able to either slow the scrolling or affect any of the images being projected. They were hard at work feeding in alternate language permutations through serried banks of translators, none of which had any effect on the displays either. The system used was unknown to Mike even with his extensive study of computer systems of codes, links, perms and quorts. The machines themselves were even fabricated from the same material of rock-metal alloy all around him. It suddenly dawned on Mike that this Quorum team seemed to be unable to interpret their own system ..... unless of course it was not their system either!

Without warning, as if triggered by his thoughts, the Quorum team wavered and vanished, leaving him sitting alone at the console. In a rush of soundless movement, Mike found himself surrounded by a real team of black suited beings, and this time they were all armed and pointing their weapons at him! One of their number stepped forward and removed his visor.

"Well fancy meeting you here!" growled an all too familiar voice as their leader removed his own mask. As Mike took a step forward, he felt a severe shock at the back of his neck and experienced a blinding flash of white light followed by total darkness.

CHAPTER TWELVE: FULL EXPOSURE

"Mr President Sir." The President stirred slightly and then almost immediately sat up fully awake and alert.

"Yes John, what is it?"

"There have been more lunar developments Sir. Your Emergency Committee have asked for your presence at the briefing room immediately"

Within 5 minutes, Orson and his staff were assembled in the briefing room. Mark Turner smiled as he turned to face the expectant faces of the team of experts gathered around the table.

"I believe we should all view this as it is happening" he began, directing their attention to a large holographic panel at the far end of the room. "This is real time Sir."

He motioned to his aide and the lights dimmed enhancing the detail of the projected image. It was an incredible sight. Even the familiar changed aspect of the Moon looked even more bizarre than ever. As they watched, the exposed side of the Moon appeared to be undergoing yet another metamorphosis. Like the curtains of a theatre, the newly exposed layer of the surface was visibly moving apart segment by segment.

"Enlarge that please" ordered Mark "and enhance the image."

The projection zoomed in, or rather expanded outwards, filling the room with the image as it did so. It showed the "shutter effect" clearly in action, leaving a black void as the only result where the shutters had once been.

"How long has this process been underway?" asked the President.

"Only for the last 20 minutes or so Sir. Each segment takes approximately 4 minutes to move completely aside, so far 10 kilometres have been exposed." answered Victor. "At the same time, we have seen a quickening in the expulsion of the lunar surface segments, an acceleration rate that will clear the surface of over half the surface of the Moon within less than a week."

"Have we received any further radio transmissions, radar images, from our own people or anyone else for that matter?"

"No Sir. All we have observed are the actions you see here. It is quite unbelievable. Those segments are precisely engineered and controlled by some power source we can't even register. This construction is simply beyond our comprehension; the sheer scale itself is impossible. This is our planet's Moon for Christsake! Who or what has the power to do all of this? All our instrumentation, advanced as it may be, has failed to detect any indication of the source of control, or even the means of control" Victor was visibly shaken and affected by the developing scenes in front of them.

"Easy now Victor. Let's concentrate on those aspects of our situation we can address and affect. Mark, how far advanced are the preparations to counter any potential hostile actions from up there?" Orson knew he had to act fast to ensure the feeling of panic and helplessness did not spread further. He was concerned about the apparent weakness of his Second in Command at such an early stage in the affair.

"At this moment Sir, our entire arsenal of Stellar Class missiles is undergoing recalibration and programming. We have calculated the permutations and sequences required to obliterate the entire mass up there should it prove necessary."

"And repercussions, casualties the environment, how will they be affected?"

"There will be relatively minor damage as far as we can tell, mostly confined to the coastal areas and populations from flooding. The dust cloud however if not totally annihilated could cause weather changes leading to potential famine and starvation for our poorest regions."

"That is not acceptable Mark. We consider this option only as the ultimate resort and only if we have irrefutable proof of an aggressive hostile attack. Agreed? Right get me more options and let's improve on what we have got so far. Let's not be rushed into anything as fatal as this until we are 110% CERTAIN!"

"But Sir....." Mark wanted to strike first but Oscar knew his style only too well.

"I know how you feel Mark," he said holding up his hands to stem the flow of protest, "but let's not go down as the chumps who kicked up a dust storm over a friendly UFO. out of ignorance?"

"OK. We will continue to scan all frequencies, all channels, all wavebands for any kind of message or signal. Concentrate on the transmissions already received. Take them to pieces and find a key so we can at least respond. Maybe that's what is expected of an intelligent race from whoever it is. Liaise with Victor; use whatever resources you need. This is now a top priority."

"We're doing that already Sir as a matter of routine. By the way there was one other development. When we were cleaning up the message transmitted to the Council, we identified a power spike under it. It was another signal aimed in the direction of the very first message received from some astropoint beyond the scope of our most sophisticated scanner range. We don't know the destination of the message, nor its content. We do know it was the same length as the one we ourselves received."

Mike was dreaming. In his head was the last image he'd seen on the screens in the computer shack. He was looking at the sequence of images, plans of what he interpreted now as the framework of the interior of the Moon. An arrangement of concentric layers of up to 20 levels of depth each sequence a part of a neighbouring ring of similar circles overlapping each other and encircling the entire satellite. At the centre of each of the layered spheres were banks of what he interpreted as dampening devices, but on a scale he had thought would be impossible to create. Other drawings of power plants and grid lines of connections and control centres assailed his unconscious thoughts. He began to feel he could grasp the concept of the puzzle but again and again the purpose eluded him. He did however realise that his attention was somehow being drawn to a minor detail within the complexities of the images. In a small often-repeated image of what must have been the centre of the entire design, a dull red light was pulsating steadily.

He concentrated again on the overall design, trying to zoom out to gain a better overall picture. There was something in the shapes and arrangements of the components telling him he should recognise what it was.

Almost without warning he returned to full consciousness, the images still fresh in his mind replaced at once by the loathsome face of Paul Gregot. Unable to move he looked down to find he had been stripped of the black suit and now lay on his back manacled at wrists and ankles to a cold black slab.

"So, our intruder awakes at last! How nice to see you again Michael."

Mike turned his head slowly to the side, trying to ignore the shooting pains in his neck, no doubt the after effects of whatever they had used on him. Paul Gregot was sitting at a chromed console regarding him as if he were nothing but an irritating insect specimen, staring at him in his usual arrogant way over the carefully manicured hands supporting a generous but chiselled chin Since they had last met, Mike could see that he had lost none of the smugness, and that he still oozed his own lugubrious brand of oily smoothness he had long claimed as his own particular style. Rick's lieutenant looked every inch the cold hard schemer that he was, only in the harsh light of the room, his good looks took on a sinister aspect, deliberately staged of course to cause the maximum effect.

'So, I was right' he thought. 'If Paul is here then so is Rick.' Paul seldom left the other man's side for any length of time. Rick relied heavily on this man's supposed superior intellect if not his physical power also. A rare breed, Paul Gregot had both the superior intellect of a high IQ, but bizarrely also possessed the body of a modern day gladiator. His strength and body definition were a legend in sporting circles apparently, long before applying his intellect to the modern commercial world. He was not averse to using whichever characterisitic gave him the ultimate advantage.

"You have the most annoying habit of poking your nose in where you shouldn't. I thought we'd cured you of that failing once and for all when we all said those fond farewells to dear old Pop!" Paul sneered in mock sympathy and almost allowed himself to smile for once.

"You bastard Gregot" hissed Mike. "Always the same story with you. Weaselling your way into positions you don't merit because of a freak of a birth that by rights should never have happened. So superior when the odds stack up in your favour, I've yet to see you perform when you haven't got the rest of your cronies doing your dirty work. You're nothing but a yellow backed ape's excuse for a man!"

No longer smiling now, Paul got up and crossed over to Mike's side barely concealing his anger at the insult and obvious challenge. His fury showed only too clearly in his eyes as he glared down at the helpless man on the slab.

"Take great care Michael!" he said using the full name as an added barb. "You are hardly in any position to cross swords with me now are you?" he glanced up and nodded at a black clad operator at the console. Mike winced in pain as a searing arc of white light exploded beneath his eyelids. "I am going to enjoy every minute of this exquisite encounter with you."

"Like I said, a yellow backed ape and a fairy to boot......."

This time a rock hard fist laid him out cold in temporary respite at what was shaping up to be a long drawn out torture session. He was not allowed the comfort of unconsciousness for long as he was jolted back to face the reality again.

"Let's just get down to business shall we?" grinned Paul obviously relishing the prospect of an easy victim. "I'm going to find out just how much you think you know about our little venture down here. Whether that becomes a pleasant experience or not depends on you. Nobody knows you're here by the way so no thoughts of rescue, not even daddy's girl Jasmine this time. Think on that. I have to leave right now, my Lord and Master is calling for my expertise yet again. But just in case you think I'm bad mannered enough to leave my guest unattended think again. My Quorum team will keep you amused I'm sure! I personally programmed them you know. Great inventor your dad -- Bless him! If you show any signs of flagging they'll be there to keep your attention. They have a whole series of nasty little experiments they're just itching to get started with. So go on, be my guest, enjoy!"

As Paul theatrically exited the room obviously deciding it worthless to continue his straight charade for his benefit, Mike realised that as far as Paul was concerned, he'd been written out of the whole equation as soon as he'd been captured. He recoiled in horror at the extent of his hatred for another human being. He had a suspicion he was going to have a great many more reasons to hate him even more before too long. As he reached the doorway Paul paused and returned to the head of the slab. He bent down and whispered one short barely audible word in Mike's ear before standing up and blowing him a kiss. Mike struggled helplessly against the restraints ands snarled at him.

"You will get yours Paul and I'll be the one to bring your miserable little excuse for a life to a very premature end. You lay one hand on her and I swear the pieces left won't bear any resemblance to your miserable body!"

"Oh I think not dear boy, Ta Ta!" Chuckling to himself, his tormentor finally left the room, leaving Mike to his fate as though it was just routine business

Looking to his left, the promised Quorum team sat patiently, presumably waiting as part of the torture to keep him guessing when and how they would begin. As he watched one of the team of 6 got up and moved out of vision. 'This is the start then' he thought to himself, running through his memory for any clues on how to escape this position. Whilst bracing himself for the first strike, he heard the characteristic sounds of shut down and was even more surprised to see the bank of blank figures waver and disappear. Next the chrome shackles at his wrists and ankles retracted. Only when the black clad figure at the console removed his visor could he believe his luck.

"Jack!"

Their first priority was easily sorted. Jack provided a spare black uniform for Mike. A quick search of their immediate surroundings showed that they were not under any kind of surveillance. Obviously the place had not been designed as a detention centre. Nonetheless they beat a hasty retreat back to Jack's hideout, nothing more elaborate than a storeroom. There was a row of the now familiar black suits on one side, the source of Jack's gift and other items of clothing, materials, tools and other boxed equipment all neatly labelled and stacked. At the far end of the spacious store stood a row of transports, similar in design and construction to the machine that Mike had arrived on, but sleeker and more powerful looking. Beyond the confines of the room, Mike pointed out more banks of cryogenic tanks.

After describing all that had happened since they lost contact on the surface Jack went on to explain how he had fared since first encountering the "black suits" as he affectionately called them. He had undergone several interrogations before the one witnessed by Mike. When he awoke from his enforced sleep, he had found the note in his hand. Galvanised into action he had waited for the return of one of his captors and once he had been unshackled for an apparent move to somewhere else, he skilfully overpowered him with ease. As a qualified instructor of ancient martial arts, Jack had him unconscious and trussed up in a matter of minutes. On taking the man's suit, he told Mike that he was convinced they were humans. Mike and Jack quickly debated the possibilities including the puzzle of the language, the equipment and not least of all the entire operation under the lunar surface come to that. Even though Mike had found the link with Paul and Rick's involvement, he was still convinced that there was a greater purpose to be found. Mike described the schematics he'd seen, the odd looking equipment and the technology needed to make this thing function. Their final conclusion to the discussion was, they were still none the wiser.

On his way to where they now found themselves, Jack described several rooms he had crossed to end up at the "torture chamber". The last one had been filled with bustling activity and equipment of great diversity and complexity, none of which made any sense to Jack with his inexperience. His pre-occupation for his own safety overrode any other considerations in this hostile environment, trying to keep as low a profile and act as naturally as he could, he had had little time for detailed examination of any of the equipment. He also noted that those around him seemed to be out of place as well, none of his comrades looked as though they were fully aware of what they were supposed to be doing, echoing Mike's observation of the Quorum team at the computer station. Everybody so far had been giving the impression of searching for instructions of some kind and none seemed fully competent with the technology. It was more reminiscent of students at a tech college comparing notes and observations than the running of an efficient plant of machinery they should have expected to find.

It was fairly easy to follow their activities and blend in without arousing too much suspicion until he had managed to work his way around to the other side of the chamber and slipped unobserved into the corridor beyond. As there had been only one corridor in and one corridor out of this area, Jack's choice had been made easy.

Beyond the chamber and about 50 metres along the corridor, he had found an ante chamber full of banks of computers and monitors. This sounded pretty much the same set up as the one Mike himself had found, possibly even the same one. The same displays were running here as those described by Mike and Jack reckoned it to be a control centre too – of what he didn't know. Mike asked about the pulsating red light he'd observed but Jack had not had the time to get too close to the displays themselves. Before very long he had heard the approach of a team of "black suits". With no way out of the room, he had scrambled to the top of the bank of monitors and laid down flat. Provided nobody looked up, he was safe from discovery. Three of the team carried in a solid looking metal box. It had an observation casing displaying a pair of startling blue eyes. He recognised it as a variant of the kind of Quorum team containment tank the company used. Once the team were deployed and seated at their workstations, one of the crew appeared to brief the leader of the Quorum team. Once the trio of "blackies" had left the room, the Quorums began their task. From the activity involved and the amount of non-verbal cross referencing going on between them, Jack guessed that they were also struggling to make sense of the display content. After a time Jack bored of observing little activity, turned his attention to the monitors. There was something familiar about the series of images shown which he felt he ought to recognise. He almost had it when he was distracted by movement below him.

One of the "black suits" had entered the room and seemed surprised to find the Quorum team in place working at the stations. He sat down at one of the consoles and examined the screen before him. Jack had only just managed to resist the temptation to call out a warning as another team of "black suits" appeared, seemingly alerted somehow by the Quorum team to a stranger in their midst. As the Quorum team were removed the six armed "blackies" stealthily surrounded the by now lone figure weapons at the ready. When their leader removed the black visor from the lone figure at the console, Jack almost gave himself away a second time as he recognised Mike instantly. As soon as they carried away Mike's' slumped figure, Jack took the opportunity to come down from his perch and followed them at a safe distance. He traced them along the first deserted corridor, neatly falling into step behind a column of paramilitary types who appeared from another passageway to his left in front of him. As he reached the door to the "torture room", taking in the scene as the file passed by, he slipped away from the line and found a dark passage where he had waited until Paul had left, still wearing the look of triumph as he went.

"You said you recognised the patterns" Mike prompted.

"Yeah that's right. Well not recognised them for what they actually are obviously. I used to be a very good Minataurian; you remember the game the Olympiad outlawed as mentally oppressive? The screen seemed to bear a close resemblance to the classic opening sequence to the game. This whole structure must be based on the same design. Now that is really weird. It's on a much grander scale of course but as you know that game is also based on a series on concentric circles within circles and includes chambers of various elements of the game. The whole concept was designed around the legends of some lost civilisation in Earth's forgotten past, you remember? Atalic….Atalis…..Atlantis yeah that's it the ancient defence system. I studied ancient civilisations at college and because of the association with the games, that part really stuck in my head."

"If my memory serves me right, wasn't there a final chamber at the centre of the maze, the lair of the beast?"

"That's right, what are you thinking Mike?

Mike thought for a few moments. "Jack, I've got to go back to a monitor and take another look at the plan. There is a definite significance in that pulsating light. I don't know what it represents but then neither do any of those goons. The fact that Gregot is here tells me they must be his men which explains why they all act like they don't belong here. If we can track it down before them, it could be a case of 'X' marks the spot!"

"OK boss! What's the plan?"

" First off, I've got to recover my gear. Can you guide me back to where those guys zapped me?

"Sure Mike, no problem. All we've got to do is walk back through the workstation across a room heaving with blackbacks go to the far side of the room and stroll along a kilometre of corridor......"

"OK, OK I get the picture. Are you up for a diversion?""

"Yup!"

"How fast can you run?"

By the time Mike retrieved his gear and returned to the Dome again, it sounded and looked like all hell had broken loose. The vehicles they had found in the storeroom had proven to be fairly simple in operation. A simple toggle switch activated a hidden power source. The familiar hum of a magno electric motor made Jack smile. This was going to be a piece of cake! He and his friends back on Earth used to race the local shopping buggies, not dissimilar to these machines during the summer breaks at the local supermarket mall, much to the annoyance of the local cops. They'd turn up at the shopping estate to find 20 or more of the carts linked together and programmed to snake their way around the aisles and surrounding pedestrian walkways which had been activated as a power grid. He and the guys would sit and watch in a study of innocence as they watched the efforts of the local law enforcers to stop the runaway trains. Because the conductor loops were underground and the only way to access them was through the very passageways the train would randomly roam, the only way to stop them was to cut the power to the entire city grid, bringing the entire city to a grinding halt in the process. Although they were often suspected, nobody could prove it was them, and nobody knew how it was done either.

Once he had figured out the basic power delivery system, it was relatively easy to programme the simple machines to form a train and randomly roam the passageways within the chamber along the invisible power tracks. Everyone was forced to leave their workstations to avoid serious injury from the unstoppable transports. It suited their purposes well as, to all intents and purposes, anybody working there could have accidentally started the thing off without knowing. Mike joined Jack at one of the banks of machinery obscured from view of the corridor.

"Over there Mike!" Jack shouted over the noise of mayhem and confusion below "That room has a complete array on line. I'll watch the door."

Now that he knew what he was looking for, Mike quickly found the projected image of the map he had seen before. He took the vidian camera from his belt and scanned the picture, zooming out from the centre to get the whole display on record for later analysis. He shut off the recorder and scanned the picture with his eye. The dull glowing spot was still evident. This time however the pace of the pulsation was different from the last time he had seen it. It was now beating every 6 seconds. Previously it had been a leisurely 30 seconds. There had to be significance in that he figured.

Leaving the crazy noise of the chamber behind them riding in the one vehicle Jack had not "nobbled", they travelled for 10 minutes in peaceful silence. They were tense and worried in case they encountered any other traffic, but their luck held. They reached a major junction where Mike tapped Jack on the shoulder. He killed the power and the vehicle smoothly halted. They flipped up the top and climbed out

"Let's see what we have got," he said as he set up the portable vidcam and set the image to maximum display on 3D.

"Each of these star shapes represents one outer reception chamber. These inner chambers must be like the one back there, you see all the conductors and grid lines fanning out from each one like a web. If we follow the logic of your corridors, the interconnections must eventually lead to the inner core right to the source of that signal or device. That's the next piece of the puzzle. All of the interconnecting corridors, no matter where you start from eventually lead to that centre. Obvious when you think about it logically." Mike smiled at the result thankful for the younger man's perception of the maze concept.

"Taking any of these chambers as our starting point then," said Mike, "means that this would be our route pattern, rather like programming in a journey back home?" he ventured tracing a line to the pulsing light.

"Basically correct, yes. But this is a 2D image, and what we are facing is a 3D maze. That and the scale of the thing and even using this vehicle as our transport we would never get there in under a month of travel time."

"Of course you are overlooking the "supercar" factor" smiled Jack. Noting Mike's quizzical expression he continued. "While we have been basically cruising on "autopilot", I've been checking this honey over, you know flicked a couple of switches just to get a feel for things, no don't worry, I knew from the configuration they had nothing to do with the propulsion system. What the screen showed was very interesting. It displayed an exact replica of your map there. On this one it shows you a logical set of instructions for loading in a course of your choice. Another display gives me options for various speeds. I think we found an afterburner with boosters here!"

"I always figured you as a basic grease monkey! Do you also happen to know exactly where we are?"

"Right here to be precise." said Jack indicating a bright white dot on the edge of the complicated looking map.

"Lay in course and speed Mr Kidd!"

"Aye Aye Captain" Jack responded mimicking Mike's lightened mood.

CHAPTER THIRTEEN: HOME TRUTHS

Jasmine awoke shivering involuntarily. It was not just from the effects of the Quorum tank, she was used to that. It was what she had observed from the containment tank that had initially heartened and then horrified her at the same time.

She shuddered as her memory "playback" replayed all that had gone on in front of her containment field tank. The eyes when stored recorded everything within their field of vision and retained the images for the host to view on their return to normal form. She did not enjoy the experience of the Quorum effect. It always left her feeling drained and nauseous on her return. She had only agreed to provide her skills this time at the request of her father, desperate to secure the answer to the current crisis, and there was nobody better qualified than she.

Seeing that Mike was indeed safe was her euphoria, seeing him captured and subjected to the brutal methods of Paul Gregot was her despair. She knew of his dark side of course and how ruthless he could be with anyone he regarded as an enemy of or a threat to the Corporation, 'or rather to his position within it' she thought to herself. She was powerless to intervene on his behalf, and the Quorum duty had taken her away from the situation altogether.

The visions she had recalled prompted her own personal memory recall. She remembered in vivid detail; the night she and Mike had finally separated and effectively the end of their marriage; Mike, consumed with grief and a little the worse from one of his regular drinking sessions, storming into her father's office in the middle of a briefing to his staff, including her; that look of absolute hatred on his face as he had lunged at Rick was unforgettable. Forcing Rick down to the level of the desk, grabbing him by the throat his face almost touching Rick's, he had openly accused him directly of Tom's murder. If it hadn't been for Paul Gregot's intervention at that point, she was certain Mike could have killed her own father right in front of her. Paul himself came close to killing Mike in turn, as his powerful vice-like grip tightened around Mike's neck. Only her pleading and pounding on Paul's back had prevented the unthinkable, but then only at an almost imperceptible nod from Rick had Paul backed off. Mike was barred from ever setting foot in Rick's office ever again. As he left unapologetic, he swore to exact a more brutal death for Rick than the one his father had suffered.

The investigation into Tom's death had been as thorough and impartial as possible, as befitted a man of such esteem and stature. There was no evidence of any involvement or wrong doing on the side of the corporation; her father or Paul Gregot come to that, which made Mike's accusation so strange and out of character. He was many things but he was not prone to falsely accusing either friend or enemy without cause. Tom's death was finally attributed to tech failure and a verdict of misadventure was pronounced in closing the case. This did nothing to satisfy Mike who openly and publicly vilified Rick at every opportunity. Despite her deep love for him she could not accept his blind conviction in his belief. Eventually she was forced to choose between the two of them - she chose Rick.

She remembered the look of malevolence in Paul's eyes as he had restrained Mike that day in the office, the same look surfacing again now just recently as he administered the restraint weapon at full charge in the computer room whilst she looked in helpless frustration from her containment tank. This time she noticed the pleasure that inflicting pain gave him, not at all the image he usually presented to the business world or in Rick's presence. It seemed that since this project had begun, his true nature was beginning to emerge. He was not the friendly and caring "uncle" she had believed him to be when she was younger.

Thinking about it, her father had also changed in subtle ways since the project began. He had always been outgoing, carefree and caring, fun and compassionate about life, people, and the future. Lately he had shown a morose, brooding and inward looking attitude she had not noticed before. His love for her was unchanged of course, but they seemed to argue more over trivial issues and any concerns she expressed were summarily dismissed as insignificant. Mostly she could explain this away as part of the cost of shielding such a secretive and vital project from the world at large. She kept her deepest concerns about him to herself, telling herself fatigue and stress were the main culprits.

The Moon project was the most top-secret project ever undertaken by the Corporation. She fully understood and supported the reasoning behind the curtain of secrecy and silence painstakingly built with absolute precision leaving an elite few who knew the full extent of their activities up here. Even so, she was not a party to every detail herself and was not even sure that she knew its ultimate objective. There were of course the obvious signs of the strain of the last few weeks, his hair was greyer and thinner, lines on his face even his manner in private moments could be described as furtive almost. He disguised his concerns well in public, but she knew him far too well to be fooled by the act. He was a worried man.

The turbulent events of the last few days and the reawakened closeness she felt again for Mike flooded back with a vengeance. During their intimate moments together aboard his ship she had caught him more than once silently weeping in his sleep. She knew instinctively that he was still haunted by his unfinished business. She had loved Tom every bit as much as Mike, and mourned his death alongside her husband with genuine sorrow. This she tempered however with an increasing dismay and anxiety over his wild accusations and fantasies of espionage and sabotage. She had hoped the demons would have been well and truly exorcised by now. If there was ever the remotest chance of them rekindling their love and passion for each other that barrier would have to be conquered one way or another. This would appear to be an impossible task, as she had gathered from his journals as he slept a long overdue sleep in the aftermath of their lovemaking, which revealed that he was in pursuit mode yet again. He had uncovered further evidence, which he believed to be conclusive in his bid for the truth and justice for his father's death. The encryption code defeated her best efforts and she could only hope that he was not about to launch yet another unjustified attack on Rick. His coded reference mark "Lianne" was tantalisingly enigmatic though, and she kept it in her head as a reminder to keep searching for a clue, any clue to help him if she could. How she wasn't at all sure of, but it made her feel closer to him somehow. Further examination of his personal log had thrown up no new references or entries under that name, but then he was a master of codes and encryption, or had been when he was part of the Corporation. She could not help but begin to feel some inner doubts, gnawing away at her inside. There must be something he knew driving him on this way. For now though he was in no position to do anything unless she could intervene.

Her thrill at being accepted by Rick to join the inner sanctum of the company and the Lunar project itself at the time of the death and her break up with Mike had been the exact tonic she had needed to shake off her own depression and sadness at losing both her friend and her lover. She had been able to throw herself heart and soul into every aspect of this mind-blowing discovery, the result of one of Rick's infamous informal "jaunts" on one of the early exploratory landings looking for mineral deposits. What began with the sudden realisation that mankind, standing on the threshold of stellar travel, was a few thousand years late into the game, was overshadowed by the evidence of superior technology and engineering prowess here beneath the surface.

She had been swept along in the euphoria of her unique position. To be invited to participate at the heart of man's greatest secret, it had been easy to accept the vow of silence imposed as the price of her ticket on the ride. More so when details of a civilisation phenomenally more advanced than their own were being exposed with each new discovery they had encountered. Exposure at this stage would have led inevitably to a circus affair as everyone scrambled to stake their claims on the Moon as the latest in the "theme park" syndrome that passed for progress in certain scientific circles on Earth.

All that had been before these latest significant events especially the revelation of the true nature of the satellite itself. Though they themselves had probably triggered the unfolding spectacular transformation up on the surface, the whole team had been caught unaware and unprepared for the outcome. Knowledge and explanations had been their driving force, but now they faced a serious twist of events which meant the time of unobserved activity and secrecy was over and a new phase had most definitely begun.

So far with the small force of 20 of Rick's most trusted staff, they had located 12 command centres. The ancient installations proved to be still functioning and bore a striking similarity to the technology of their own computer driven world. They found it relatively easy to power up each of the centres in turn, the last one being the site of Mike's "arrest". As in each of the other stations already activated, they could read the displays but seemed unable to initiate or impose any function commands, however many banks of Quorum team decoders they applied to the task, or so they had thought up until now. With the spectacular events on the surface coinciding with the progress down below, there was always the chance that a random command had initiated an automatic response. The possibility spurred the whole team on in their search for a solution and answers to these unforeseen increasing and alarming developments.

That was the fundamental and only reason Jasmine had volunteered to provide herself as a host for the Quorum team. Her personal discomforts were her contribution to the urgent requirements of the expedition. Now she had the added burden of having witnessed an unexpected and unwelcome side to their goal and it scared her more than anything else she had ever seen. "Uncle" Paul, the gentle giant in whose hands she had often literally entrusted her own safety and her life was now a monster and unrecognisable dangerous beast. Anybody who could enjoy so obviously the power of pain and suffering of others and yet pretend to be such a caring and over-protective person was a danger indeed. That it had been Mike suffering at his hands had been one factor too much. So much so that she now found herself questioning everything the Corporation had stood for and meant to her. For certain it was not conducive to the goals she and Rick talked about at length over their cosy suppers at night.

Her rescue from the destruction of the Lunar base had been real enough to remind her of how precarious they were. She had more than enough to thank Mike for in reality, her own life for God's sake. She was only too aware that she had been denying to herself for too long now just how much she had missed his understated strength of character and that feeling of total security whenever he was around. Whatever the circumstances of his intrusion into their secret, he did not merit such brutality. 'Well I'll put a stop to that if nothing else' she decided to herself. Fully recovered now, she dressed quickly and headed straight for her father's study. As he neared his door, she could hear raised voices -- her father and Paul!

"So, you've known the true purpose of this installation all along" she heard her father say "and played me for a fool from the start? Think again Paul, you haven't got the savvy. You forget who it was got us here, who found the way through the outer layers to reach these workings. I don't see any investment from you in this at all. The only "power" you have is all-corporate, and I control that. This discovery will eventually be for the benefit of Mankind as we intended all along, not for you alone, myself or any other reason. You accepted that as I did from the outset, nothing has changed."

"My dear Richard, do you really think you are in charge here? Look around and open your eyes. All the key personnel are loyal to me, they obey me, they are trained by me, they belong to me and do as I command …not you. I will do as I see fit, I will assume control from hereon in!"

"You can't do that!" said a defiant Rick. From her vantage point Jasmine could see they were only brave words. Rick had little option but to listen in silence to the torrent of abuses Paul now rained down upon him as he sat coolly with the muzzle of a wicked looking weapon held just in front of his face.

"Just give me the word Paul," said Johan without taking his eyes off Rick. "Let's get this over and done with!"

"Easy now Johan." Paul restrained his ever-eager lackey with a withering stare. "We still need him and his brain for some time yet, and the co-operation of that bitch of a daughter too. Without them we don't stand to gain as much as we do with them, so let's not scramble those cells for a while yet."

Jasmine had seen enough. If ever she had needed Mike's help it was now. Quietly she backed away from the door turning as she did. As she got up and began to run, she almost failed to see the black suited security guard until it was too late. Ducking under his arm she thought she had made it, then came the sting of pain at the back of her neck, the white searing light and then darkness

CHAPTER FOURTEEN: HIGH STAKES

"Just remember Rick, Old Tom would be alive today but for your lax security. You were Security Director after all and you failed miserably in the execution of that role. You were his friend and his shield. He trusted you and you let him down."

There was no mistaking the mockery in Paul's spiteful outburst. He refused to let this challenge go unanswered.

"You know damned well I had no part in his death you bastard. We all know the conclusion was espionage related, but I know for a fact there was an insider at work. A little more digging will reveal just how, and more to the point exactly who had the knowledge to bypass all the security protocols we'd created together."

"That may well be the case, but for now, everybody holds you personally accountable for his demise. You may not have actually cut the gas charged supply, but your negligence cost your friend dear." sneered Paul.

"So! That's as good as any confession anyone could hope for!" Rick spat back at him. "No details have ever been released of how the death was engineered to look like an accident. Apart from the High Commission Investigator and myself, nobody was informed about the outcome of the investigation, which means that the only other person aware of that fact is the killer himself. Congratulations Paul!" Now Rick was mocking him with a slow hand-clap as he made a move towards him. "And you can bet I'll take great pleasure from seeing you get your just desserts!" he hissed through clenched teeth as he faced Paul.

Without flinching, Paul stared him out. "Well my friend, it seems to me that your usefulness in all this has come to a sudden end after all. We have no further need of you." Paul took a step back turned and Johan fired his stun pistol directly into Rick's face. At that distance the effects were hideous causing even Paul himself to flinch. As the structure of his face imploded, death was instantaneous. Before the body had even slumped to the floor, Paul turned and left the room ordering Johan over his shoulder to clean the mess up as he went, almost as if he was ordering a beer.

In truth the incident shook Paul, not the killing of course, no feelings there. No he was worried that he was losing control of the situation. Rick had come to his conclusions a little bit late, but still too soon for Paul. There was so much more to be accomplished if their final goal were to be realised --- and now he would have to go the last stretch on his own. Rick had guessed all along that there had been somebody on the inside. It would not have needed too much imagination to establish his link with the "originals". Up to this point, he had been adept at shielding his true identity. He could not, would not compromise that yet --- not at any price! Too bad, he had liked Rick's attitude and personality. He could almost believe he had been more like "them" than he was his own kind. He had made sure of his own value almost as soon as he realised others of his kind were being re-awoken. He dispatched his "companions" as easily and without thought as he had dispatched his sponsor and the man responsible for his pleasant life style. 'No matter!' he thought to himself 'Once the cycle is completed, all power will be mine.' The key question of course was the events going on up top, and how they would impact on his long laid plans and schemes ---- and that was beyond his direct control. He determined to have few regrets about Rick. For most of their association the man had been a constant source of irritation. Now that their shared goal was within reach, the sanctimonious do-gooder for all his tough talk, had just been emotional excess baggage. 'An accident, skilfully arranged of course' he mused to himself. Then he realised he could just as easily arrange for the perfect deception to suit their purpose. 'Dead men tell no tales --- or women for that matter!' He grinned to himself as he contemplated his next move. 'Now to sort out our other friends.' His pace quickened as he approached the intersection and took the diagtravtube downwards to where the passage ended at a hatchway halfway along the wall at the end.

As usual the mutes sat in the same expressionless stance as he had left them. Motionless, impassive, barely registering his presence with a flicker of recognition, the three beings sat as if in prayer, hands joined fingers on lips. Paul sat before them and briefly mimicked their pose to gain their attention. He had discovered their mental abilities were less than those of an average 6 year old. At first he had feared some brain damage had occurred during their early attempts at revitalisation which had impaired their knowledge. However he now believed that these three like the others before them were actually cloned that way on purpose, as no brighter subjects had been retrieved from one of the series of cryogenic banks. They were most definitely not the engineer or scientist class responsible for the station and its functions, of that he was now more than sure. 'More than likely the garbage detail!' he had scoffed to himself. None of these three had responded to any of the schematic images they had copied from the mainframe computer of the satellite. Only when basic images of the Earth and the Moon had appeared had there been any inkling of intelligence and then from only one of the trio. He had mimed an explosion of the Earth and then gestured to the Moon by cupping his hands to surround the image. This had convinced the Earth team that they were dealing with a weapon of enormous power and energy, but without understanding its ultimate purpose or objective. Rick had restrained him then from more severe and extreme methods of extracting information. Left to their own devices they followed what appeared to be a pre-programmed route from the chamber to the storage chambers where, with great efficiency, they had proceeded to activate lighting, heating and plumbing arrangements. However when faced with any other forms of technology, especially the computer banks, they just blanked out and sat still. They were definitely not the creators of their race. They were however his one fragile link to the technology around them, and he wasn't going to let them off lightly! He began by greeting them in the slow hand signals they had devised as the only common language. Whenever they spoke amongst themselves, they spoke in a series of wheezes and clicks, their mother tongue obviously, and one which was lost on him. He had never encountered it himself, confirming his thought that they were of a low class minority.

"Hail Person One" he began

"Hail"

"Much movement above. Why?"

"Not"

"Can halt Person One, Person Two, Person Three?" he pointed at each of them in turn

"Not. Boom!" again came the mimed explosion

"No! Not Boom! How?"

A dismissive shrug of the shoulders indicated the predictable outcome of the conversation.

"How? Other than you Four, Five Six?"

Again the shrug with the ceremonial punctuation which he gathered to mean "The Highest"

"Here? Here?" he emphasised the gesture trying to force a useful response.

Another shrug and a mime this time of sleeping, indicating their period of hibernation.

'Too ambiguous.' he thought. He tried once more

"The Highest. Asleep? Here?"

This time he elicited a smile and a shallow bow. 'At last something positive!'

"Show! Show!" he was signing frantically now.

"Not! Not!"

Sign language was no longer necessary now as their expressions told of real fear as their leader wilted and succumbed under the flurry of punches aimed at its fragile body until finally it slid onto the floor, a bleeding mass of shapeless matter.

"Observe and consider long!" he signed at them and abruptly left the small chamber.

===

The ride was almost surreal. If he looked through the small viewscreen, the walls of the tunnel appeared as spirals of light and dark colours punctuated only by junctions and crossways that came and went in milliseconds. He found it uncomfortable to look for too long at any one time. The effects were quite disconcerting and disorienting. If he moved away from the viewscreen, he could not feel any sensation of movement at all. From the build up of speed at the start, he guessed that they were travelling at in excess of 300kph. With no sound or motion to gauge from they could just as easily be standing still. He figured that the deceptively simple craft was heavily damped and cocooned in a force field of some sort allowing a high degree of comfort for the occupants

With literally nothing for them to do once they had adjusted the display array for their destination, all they could do was to sit back and enjoy the ride. As soon as they began to move, the keypad, screen and all other internal equipment folded away into the fabric of the craft itself. Even the internal temperature appeared to be on remote control. Mike wasn't sure that he welcomed the opportunity for further speculation on the recent events of the last few hours. He could scarcely believe he was about to enter his fifth day in this underground enigma.

Now that he knew the full scale of Paul's involvement, he could begin to piece together some of the puzzle. He had little doubt that even before their brief encounter Paul was a seriously under-estimated spoiler in the great scheme of things. His instincts told him that the rift between Rick and Tom was in large measure attributable to the arrival of this strange man on the scene. Tom himself had always viewed the sudden and subsequently omnipresence of the man at Rick's side wherever he went with a high degree of trepidation. Rick seemed to rely on him for virtually everything in the business. Paul himself had demonstrated extreme cunning and stealth in advancing his original position of consultant and advisor to one of enormous power and influence over the direction and strategy of the company, sanctioned unilaterally by Rick's specific instruction. Many times Tom had confronted Rick with specific instances of "strong-arm" tactics used to secure contracts, but Rick had always been able to talk the old man round to his way of thinking with reassurances and personal guarantees for Paul's "integrity". Inevitably, Tom was outmanoeuvred to the point where his own power base was gradually eroded away from under his nose, almost imperceptibly, his voice in the decision making processes was reduced to that of a whisper. Ultimately the situation led to a bitter split between the partners resulting in the division of the company into research under Tom's direction, and the more commercial operations under Rick.

Mike's role had been that of a go-between, liaising between the commercial operations and the research department, sometimes as a policy maker, but more often as a peacemaker. He too encountered the insidious presence of Paul at every meeting. He had determined to ignore the imposition and at first managed to avoid conflict. He could on the one hand admire the extreme intelligence of Paul's input and insight, but even then there were undertones of manipulation and opportunism lurking behind every strategy, every adjustment in the running of the company. Rick's day to day grip on the affairs of the company were gradually reduced and the decision making process left more and more to his right hand man, ostensibly to take the pressure of the business away from Rick, leaving him free to be as creative as he wanted. To Mike's eyes it looked more like a subversive take-over attempt. Whenever he got the chance alone with Rick, he would express his concerns, only to be told to mind his own business, and that he was far too inexperienced to understand the nuances of the game plan. Rick regarded Paul's contribution as vital to the future success of the company. Nothing Mike could say or do would alter his total belief in and support for Paul. Finally when Mike persisted and tried to present evidence of Paul's handiwork at first hand, that had been the start of the wedge that eventually led to their bitter split. Paul as ever exploited the rift to its full potential ruthlessly pursuing the goal of total destruction of their father-in-law/ son-in-law relationship aside from the business connection.

Mike recalled the connection he established between the deterioration of the relationships within the company and the appointment of it as the engineering contractor for the very Lunar project itself. With the respect of the World Council for the company as his ace card, Paul had successfully presented a compelling case for their sole appointment in charge of the project as only he could. Manipulative, coercive and persuasive, he had charmed and cajoled the members of the council to see the vision through his own eyes and burning ambition with the promise of technological advance and global wealth enhancement as their carrot. Now that he was witnessing where much of the funding had been spent, he could appreciate the excessive security and furtiveness surrounding so many of the late night "secret" conferences and meetings to which even he at the beginning could not gain access.

In retrospect, he wished he had stood his ground alongside Tom and confronted the monster which had since been allowed to grow until it had enough strength and substance to strike. Its first strike had been incisive and far-reaching but above all tragic. The death of one of the founders of the organisation, and the head of its research facility had at one blow removed any remaining constraints on Rick's ambition, and robbed the company of any steadying conscience.

And now it was obvious that willingly or unwillingly, even Rick was being influenced by this spreading cancer. Exactly how much he condoned and sanctioned directly Mike could not be sure. He knew that he would be at least aware of the extent of this loathsome man's handiwork. If he didn't know before, Mike had enough direct proof and evidence to convert even the most die-hard supporter. Once he had all of the answers to this particular crisis, he was convinced he would be able to restore a modicum of sanity and turn Rick around to his way of thinking. Even if Rick and he could not personally get back to a normal relationship, Rick would not ignore the proof if it was presented to him now. Then there was Jasmine. Where did she stand in all this? It seemed obvious that her presence on the Moon was no accident. Was she involved? Did she know about all of this? He began to question and query everything he could recall in their discussions relating to the Lunar project. She and Rick had always been very close. The fact that Rick appeared to be in control of the project, the very suppression of information and knowledge of the discovery, all of the factors that led to Rick's door could just as easily lead to her door too. Had it been Rick's interference and probing down here that triggered off the events topside?

"Mike! I think we're getting near to our destination." Jack cut into Mike's thoughts suddenly followed almost at once by the appearance of restraint harnesses which automatically moulded and adjusted themselves to their bodies. All of the instruments and control panels also reappeared. Peering ahead through the viewscreen, Mike could make out the shape of what he imagined to be a terminal of some kind.

"We're being asked for some kind of signal in response to their command judging by this panel," he continued "a three digit sequence, colour coded and intermittent timing splits."

"Can you work it out?" asked Mike.

"Should be easy enough. I think it is a simple acknowledgement. I'm sending a duplicate response ...... now."

Jack hit the transmit button and was rewarded with a level single tone followed by the car moving into the docking bay. It stopped, opened and released the restraints in one smooth operation. They got out and took in the surroundings, looking for some clue as to their next move, wary and ready for anything.

"What now?" asked Jack.

The docking area was devoid of any features, the same dullish sheen on the walls indicating that it was moulded from Moon material. Their only obvious indication of a point of exit appeared to be a spiral staircase at the far end of the wall just behind the end of the track itself. It led them to a glass fronted gallery overlooking the terminal. Behind the glass they saw a row of cryogenic chambers, all fully occupied. Mike counted 12. One of them was obviously in the final stages of its cycle as it vented the contents of the interior in a cloud of vapour.

CHAPTER FIFTEEN: RUDE AWAKENINGS

Jasmine emerged from the shower frowning with the realisation that Rick had not returned her call. Normally he would have checked in on her as a matter of course after her session in Quorum status, had done since she had first begun to operate the procedure, even though she chided him for being over-protective of her. Right now she would have welcomed the attention and concern. As usual, the nausea and cramps had begun to ease and although the extremities of her vision were still a little fuzzy, she was alert and refreshed. She was anxious to hear any news about Mike. After hearing about the shambles of the chaotic events in the main chamber, she guessed it had been Mike at the root of it all. She couldn't help but wonder how he was taking all of this, and what he was feeling about her now. She knew he would be worried about her but she had to keep her solemn promise to Rick not to reveal her involvement to anybody until he agreed. That still applied, even to Mike as far as she was concerned. At least he was alive! She took some comfort from that, knowing that in sharing herself with him in the events leading up to their entry to the complex, all of her pent-up passions and feelings for him were straining to re-assert themselves. Hard as it was to deny those feelings, she had resolved to keep them on ice until this adventure reached its conclusion. Now that he had himself witnessed the amazing discovery, she wanted to share this and more with him, to win him over to their side and their goals and dreams. Mankind would hail them all as heroes when the full extent of their find was presented to the world as a total victory of man over technology if ... if .... There was still so much they did not understand and so much more to master before that day could be. The recent events topside confirmed that beyond any doubt. Devastating beyond belief, they had all been taken by surprise, nobody knew who was controlling whatever was causing the changes to take place. There was much speculation that its purpose was not benign to Earth. Earth's fate, its very existence could hang on the frantic scramble for information and knowledge taking place all around them, She felt a heavy responsibility along with an oppressive concern at the enormity of their task, and finally, who had knocked her out and why?

Dressing quickly now, she scooted down the corridors until she reached her father's quarters and knocked gently on the door. When she got no reply, she tried the door handle and pushed open the door. The room seemed to leap out at her as she slumped to her knees in disbelief and despair at the gruesome spectacle before her. Even with the hideous distorted melting of the head she recognised Rick's body immediately. He had died an agonising death, that much was obvious. Tears stung her cheeks as she crawled over to the lifeless form and cradled him in her lap. The body was cold. How long had she been out? No more than three hours she was sure. When did this happen, who would want to hurt him in this way? Why? Cold reality slapped her face and helped her back into some semblance of self control as she realised that having discovered the crime, she was now at risk from its perpetrator herself. Gently lowering him to the floor, she crawled over to the safe box and secured the only weapon she knew her father had sanctioned for the base, a stun gun. It had been one of Rick's most stringent rules that no arms were to be carried throughout the complex. Whoever the assassin was, he had defied that order already, so now the balance was restored at least.

Totally rational now she scanned the room to pinpoint the tell-tale micro-spy dot Rick had planted. It was not where she expected to find it. Somebody had been very thorough and knew the normal security measures they shared. She abandoned the search for that one and changed the scanner frequency to her own encoded signal. The feedback was instant. Her own device was still present and had been activated, Seeking out the treasured family holopic, she deftly removed a false corner and tipped the contents inside into her hand. Carefully extracting the micro receiver, she placed it securely into a pouch in her shoulder pocket for later investigation. She would have revenge, and she would have the element of surprise on her side to extract it! Before leaving the room she tenderly covered her father's body and then considered her next move. In theory Paul should have already been here. Something persuaded her not to hit the panic button to get the self-proclaimed protector to Rick's aid. Too late for that now! Until she viewed the recording, she could trust no-one.

As it was quite late in the evening, relatively speaking, there were few people about as she checked the corridor in both directions. Seeing it was clear she made to leave but stopped mid step as a brief flash of red light emitted from mid way down the door frame. Had she not been crouching down to check the corridor she would have missed it completely. She recognised it immediately as a micro laser device recently developed in the lab. It was pulsing at maximum intensity. It must have been activated when she opened the door on her way in. Whoever had murdered her father had expected her to run screaming and panicking out of the room for help. Had she done so, she would have been sliced in half. Bristling with anger at the double sleight at the stereotype "female" and the implied weakness of her character, she calmly thought through the consequences of the unfolding plot of double assassination. A scream, horrific injuries, what was the next logical step, what would they expect her to do? She retreated back into the room and looked around, a plan already forming. There was no other way she could think of, she needed to leave the room fast!

A blood-curdling scream resounded throughout the complex.

As the body separated into two pieces and hit the floor, the black visor covering the head hit ground hard and cracked. Paul was alerted through the vidcom link and smiled. "Let's go sweep up the pieces." he said.

When they got to the scene of the disturbance, a small group of workers moved aside to let him through and then began to drift back towards their work stations, curiosity sated now, how soon they seemed to lose interest when they saw him approach. Smiling in grim satisfaction, Paul surveyed his handiwork. The smile quickly faded to a scowl as he realised the severed torso was not his intended victim. Yet again, he had been thwarted in his efforts! Too late, he turned to stop the onlookers from leaving the scene. The last one turned out of sight. 'She is most certainly a clever little vixen' This, the last member of the family he had come to detest. All the frustrating years of subservience and control he had endured should have been ended with the demise of this one last obstacle. Then the empire he had helped create would have been his alone. But no! Two loose ends still needed to be dealt with, Jasmine especially. Only she knew the hold Rick had over him, and which had often been used to subdue his wilder excesses and kept him in check. He was tired of playing second fiddle. As head of the corporation, now he would command respect and obedience on his own terms. But, not yet it seemed. Jasmine knew, she knew about this and several of his other "indiscretions". Well he could take his time. She wasn't likely to get too far, her and that other distraction, Mike. "Get this cleared up and let's move the project timetable up a notch or two!" he snapped at Johann as he turned curtly on his heel and headed back towards the Control Room.

Jasmine held her composure well as she walked back with the crowd which gathered in response to her strident screams. As she had expected the laser guillotine had been set for a single charge, the device self-destructing to leave no evidence of its presence. It had been a heart rending emotion to have used her father's corpse in that way, but it had been her only means of escape. She had cringed at the ease with which the beam had sliced through the flesh and bones but quickly stepped through the doorway and ran towards the work stations at the end of the corridor. Now slipping away with the crowd for cover, she gained valuable time for herself. Once clear of the work station area she headed for the tunnels at the far end of the chamber. Taking one, she followed it for at least 1 kilometre before finding a niche in the wall where she slumped to the ground and released her burden of sorrow for the next hour.

Amid the grief and disbelief at this latest turn of events, she finally began to perceive the suppressed thought, that Mike's insight and intuition towards the Corporation, her father and Paul had all been well founded in fact. He may have been homing in on the wrong person, but his motivations were true and sure. How could she have been so easily fooled into doubting him, his foresight and integrity? And especially now when her need of him was greater than ever and he was adrift somewhere, lost and perhaps more poignantly, feeling alone and abandoned even by she herself, she had no idea of where to start looking for him. He was now her only hope for survival. She just had to track him down, find him. Although she knew she would have a lot of explaining to do, instinct told her he would understand and know what to do. But where was he and how to get to him? She felt sure the mayhem caused in the Control Room with the travel pods was his mischief for sure. It had all the hallmarks of his handiwork. The engineers had been stumped by the event. She herself had helped in the clear up operation, and had been pleased when she accounted for all but one of the transports. She was certain now that somehow Mike had escaped in it. All that she now needed to do was track it and him down. She still had a few tricks up her sleeve to help her with that. Suitably resolved and refreshed from within, she set about her new strategy and headed for the nearest transport terminal.

Mike sat mesmerised by the processes he was watching. The cryogenic process appeared to follow a conventional pattern, like any on Earth. Then, just as it appeared to be drawing to a close, two parallel vid boards on either side of the main console began to revolve at first slowly and then increasing in speed until they were almost invisible. From them there emerged a series of holographic images which seemed to illustrate the passage of time in a sequence where the Earth and Moon circled each other like sparring partners looking for the first opening. The land-mass of the Earth appeared to be different to the views Mike was used to but they were unmistakably the Earth and the Moon. As he watched the entire time representation of the images went into a kind of "fast forward" mode until it arrived at a sequence which he recognised as illustrating the recent external events preceding his presence here in this place.

"Thus was it predicted!" A metallic sounding voice

made him jump into a defensive stance as he turned to face the speaker. Standing before him was the stooped figure of an old man, shaking either from his advanced years, or from the after effects of the cryogenics operation. The figure appeared to be a man of 80 to 90 years old, stooped and with wispy grey long hair, his skin a ghostly grey, crinkled and lined with age, his fingers gnarled and bent as if racked by disease. Yet the eyes betrayed an essential vitality that seemed out of place, clear blue and alert, shining with anticipation.

"There has been a return, else I would not have been so rudely awakened from my sleep." It was as much a question as a statement. The old man went on "Where are the others?" Whilst considering the real meaning of the question, Mike realised that the man had not opened his mouth to speak. 'Telepathy?'

"Yes. Why does this puzzle you so?" the metallic sounding voice droned on. "From which Quadrant do you serve? I do not recognise your insignia! Do you not acknowledge me?" The frail old man took a step closer, almost stumbling as he approached.

Mike caught him easily and guided him to a chair at the console. "Easy now old timer! I've got you now." he soothed.

The old man stared at him curiously. "You do not use the mind communication?" he seemed confused by the sound of Mike's voice. "Where are you from? You wear the garb of my people yet you do not respond normally. Do you not know me? What of Earth? Tell me what has happened?"

The thought transmissions faded away as the stranger seemed to make a concerted effort to emulate Mike and emitted a squeaky voice from between dry lips. Although Mike had understood the meaning, the language was the one he had heard back at the Operations Room.

With a combination of hand-signals, quick sketches and sign language. Mike tried to indicate that he could "hear" the mind language but could not understand it well. The old man reached inside his suit and produced what appeared to be a miniature voice synthesiser. He keyed in a three digit code and motioned for Mike to give him a sample of speech.

"Hello! I am Mike, Engineer of Space, Citizen of Earth!"

The stranger held up his hand and worked at the keyboard for a few moments before replaying Mike's words in the strange click and grunt expression that must have been the native tongue. He smiled at the replayed message.

With great solemnity and ceremony he turned to face Mike and spoke to him again. This time Mike understood every word.

"Greetings Mike, Engineer and Citizen of Earth. My name is Dhoran, High Council Priest and Commander of Earth Sciences. You may give due reverence now!" When no adulation was forthcoming from either Mike or Jack, Dhoran continued, this time with genuine confusion and curiosity. "Forgive my rudeness and unfamiliarity with your class rituals, the levidorm process takes some moments to fully clear the system. I am most curious as to your origin and your tongue. It resembles one of our most ancient and primitive forms of language, seldom heard, if at all outside the colleges, going back before the pretoxinal age of our world. Where are you from, and why have you returned to the complex?"

Feeling strangely relaxed and safe in the company of this ancient survivor of the unknown history of the Moon, Mike put his trust and faith in his instincts. As quickly, concisely and thoroughly as he could, he ran through a brief history of mankind, their technology and ambitions, ending with a summary of their activities on the Moon. He finished with a short briefing on the events which had led them on their path to discovering Dhoran. Dhoran listened intently, impassively for over an hour as Mike presented his sketchy but generally unbiased explanation of Man's quest for knowledge. Occasionally he would rock back and forth, eyes closed in contemplation looking as though he were meditating or praying to himself, but obviously absorbing every word of the narrative as, checking with Jack now and then for verification, Mike described Earth Politics and Culture leading into the system by which their project to explore the Moon's potential had come to the dramatic events and shock of the discovery of the hidden lunar facility. Mike did not finish speaking until he recounted the adventures both he and Jack had endured after the initial Moonquake to their arrival at the terminal.

After a few minutes of silence, Mike began to wonder if Dhoran had fallen asleep. The bright alertness of the unusually pale blue eyes told him otherwise. Eventually Dhoran ended his self-imposed period of contemplation and spoke in sombre tones that carried through even the mechanical translator device.

"There is much I have to tell you and I know you are anxious to know everything. The magnitude of such revelations will require deep resource of contemplative ability. If I am to provide you with the answers you seek to resolve your immediate danger and then succeed in the greater need for your race, we must begin our preparations immediately. I sense in both of you an aura of goodness. I will trust you to watch over me as I undergo the *krolmat* once more. There is scant time for a full explanation now, when it is complete, we will talk again. Know this for now. Your race has retraced the steps that many civilisations of mankind have traced before, only to fall at this same hurdle. Now is our time to avoid the perils of that moment and continue the delayed evolution beyond the barriers of the past."

He beckoned for Mike and Jack to help him to his feet and guided them to a cubicle recessed at the back of the chamber. He entered the cubicle unaided now and sat down on a low protrusion that jutted out from the wall. As he did so a concealed translucent door closed off the cubicle isolating them from each other. An indigo glow of suffused light showed Dhoran in an upright position as a sharp blue beam appeared to scan his body from top to bottom and back in a regular cycle that appeared to be set to continue for some undetermined time.

"Well, I guess we do as he says." said Jack. "What did you make of that Mike?"

"I guess we will have to be patient and hang around to find out. Meantime we'd better prepare ourselves for any and every eventuality. If we can get here then sure as hell so can anybody else. Let's organise a surveillance operation covering the terminal."

As he spoke, Jack grabbed his elbow. "Do you hear something?"

They looked at each other and ran towards the staircase. Sure enough as if he had prophesied the event, another transport was slowly entering the terminal. He retrieved the stunner from his back-pack. The car reached the platform and halted. Nothing else happened. Mike motioned for Jack to cover the new arrival from the darkness of the track below the platform. He himself kept low, below the line of vision of the transport, breaking cover to reach it at the last possible moment. He pulled open the black canopy and thrust the stunner inside. It was empty!

Too late he sensed rather than felt the barrel of a weapon pointed at his head. He turned to face the threat slowly to find his stalker was a black suited visored figure. As he stood up and faced him, the figure crumpled and fell at his feet.

Jack stood behind the now prostrate figure smiling. "Always knew that martial arts would come in handy someday."

As they snatched the helmet and visor away the last thing they both expected was the cascade of golden hair that spilled out and around the unconscious face.

"Jasmine!"

CHAPTER SIXTEEN: REUNION

When she began to wake up, for a moment Jasmine imagined there was a beam of intense white light, which felt as though it was slicing through her skull. Her eyes fluttered open in sheer terror and panic and she thrashed about in a hopeless attempt to break free from the restraints holding her down at wrists and ankles.

"Jasmine, are you all right?" she scarcely believed her good luck as recognition of Mike's voice filtered through the fuzzy thoughts dashing around in her head. She opened her eyes fully to see him standing by her side and that was it! The floodgates opened, and with heaving shoulders and through body wracking sobs, she released all of the pent-up feelings emotions and frustrations at once, giving herself up to him completely. There was no need for talk, that would come later. For now she could relinquish all self-control secure in his strong embrace. Mike released her and held her tenderly until depleted of any further emotion she sagged into him and fell asleep. He still held her 3 hours later when she recovered sufficiently to resurface feeling purged and refreshed once again. There was no question now, no holding back as she talked to him at length, this time leaving no detail out, no secrets remaining. Even with

Jack present she felt that they had both endured too much to be denied any more the knowledge than she had. From her earliest involvement with the project, through the excavation period and all the subsequent discoveries, secrecies and subterfuges she left nothing out. Mike sat spellbound at the depth of her knowledge and involvement, confused and yet exhilarated at the scale of the operation she described and its implication for mankind.

A discreet cough brought them out of their unspeaking trance-like state.

"If indeed you have uncovered so much of my work, then perhaps you might care to illuminate us as to its very purpose?"

Mike turned around slowly, and for the second time in as many minutes sat in open mouthed amazement. Standing before him stood the unmistakable presence of the aged alien they had encountered before, except that this one appeared to have taken an intensive anti-ageing serum.

"Allow me to introduce and re-introduce myself. My name is Dhoran, Chief High Priest and Earth High Commander of Science. I am the creator of this facility, and the cause of your colleagues' bewilderment. The effects of the crolavin procedure is unknown to you? All citizens of Earth are obliged to undergo the procedure at least 3 or 4 times during their lifetime. Does that not apply to your kind?"

It was a genuine question. Extremely handsome, tanned, strong and bristling with vitality now, Mike could not help but ask the obvious.

"How did you do that?

"My friend, I will be more than happy to share this and other knowledge with you, once we have attended to the more urgent need to deter this young lady's pursuers. Look!"

The oblong view panels began to revolve again, slowly at first, almost like the old silent movies he'd watched in history lessons at school, the picture emerged as a flickering image at first, before evolving into a 3D image of faultless resolution as the screens reached operating speed. They showed the menacing image of at least three transport devices barrelling through the tunnels, presumably following the trail created by Jasmine's flight.

"Well at least that is an easy issue to resolve!" Dhoran laughed as he turned to the control panel moving his hands deftly above the array of illuminated controls changing the pattern of connections as he did so.

"That will contain them until we are ready to deal with them. They will continue to circle us in a closed link of tunnel with no harm to either themselves or us. Why do they pursue you? Are you a criminal?" Dhoran directed his thoughts towards Jasmine who had joined Mike in fascinated absorption of the images and their connection to the control Doran had imposed.

"Just like my old train-set!" chimed in Jack. "My dad gave me a toy when I was young. By setting up a motherboard on the controls, the train would follow a set pattern of travel, but my God, you altered solid rock to channel them into a continuous loop!"

"If you are to understand the nature of this grave situation we are in, and understand *our* world, you must agree to undertake a short period of enforced learning, totally safe I assure you, which will eliminate the need and your never-ending quests for knowledge in an instant. Do you agree to this?"

"How can we be sure it will cause no harm?" Jacks question sounded lame under the circumstances, but they all had the same concern.

Patiently, Dhoran explained that their very presence was witness to their tolerance of the environment and the in-built defences of the facility. "If it were not so, then we would not be holding this discussion."

"Dhoran, please give us a few moments to consider this?" asked Mike, well aware that Jasmine hovered on the edge of nervous exhaustion and needed at least some breathing space to gather her thoughts and strength before the next challenge. Even though her defences were in place and fully functional, Mike knew her well enough to interpret the signs of stress behind the mask.

"Jasmine, are you all right? I seem to have been blind for so long. I'm so sorry about your Dad, and I'm glad I was wrong about him in the end. I feel so frustrated that my stupidity and stubbornness drove us apart the way it did and ......"

"Mike, Mike, I'm just so washed out right now. I'm hurt and sad and angry and so mixed up. I know exactly how you must have felt when Tom was killed, and I don't blame you for suspecting Rick was to blame. That's the way Paul manipulated it. Now that we both know that for sure, it changes everything. I've got confirmed evidence of that, and together we can defeat him and have our revenge... together this time." She gave him a look he'd almost forgotten, and suddenly realised the old magic was back again as though it had never been away.

"You're right as usual. Hey listen, what do you make of all this, Dhoran and all this stuff? I think we have little choice but to trust him, he seems to be on our side at least. But can you take any more right now, are you ready for battle?"

"The way I see it, we have little choice" she replied wistfully. "We were getting close, but this guy is the closest thing to unravelling this enigma, and the only solid evidence of the race which put this thing here. If we are going to find the answer to the question, it must be through him. We cannot guess who or what stands to gain from all of this. Dhoran might just be the elusive key we have been missing since we uncovered this complex. All anybody does know for certain is that Earth is endangered by something or somebody. Paul acts like he knows, but he doesn't. He's just as blind as any of us. I'm with you on this. Let's get some answers!"

The rejuvenated Dhoran was excited   more excited than he could ever recall in his long existence. He had good cause. Everything was as he had anticipated. His only error was that of time itself. He paused as he glanced briefly at the new arrival with amusement and satisfaction. Then with the merest hint of a nod to nobody but himself, he re-applied himself with enthusiasm, refocusing his attention in full to the colourful and complicated array displayed in all its multicoloured splendour. With grim foreboding his instincts told him that the next few hours were likely to be crucial in the execution of his long laid and long overdue plans. With the assistance of these three fresh minds, he was even more certain of the outcome than ever before. They provided him with the last link in the scheme, if only by the fact of their presence and their manual help alone. He considered himself fortunate indeed on that count! Having finished his calibrations at the desk, he turned to face them now, deciding to speak in deference to their own custom.

"You know from what you have seen and experienced on this satellite that these "workings" as you call them, have existed throughout all of your entire history of Earth and beyond. What you will not know is that this knowledge covers but a bare fraction of the dominance of mankind on planet "Earth" as you know her. There have been many and several civilisations before yours, some more advanced others less so. Each of these has in turn succumbed to the laws of physics at the end to be destroyed and be reborn through global devastation. This last time, in my lifetime, we were close to removing the threat of annihilation forever. We had the answer in our grasp, or so I thought. Through our mastery of the mysteries of molecular behaviour and atomic time mass stress computations, my research unearthed the tell tale signs of the cause of these cataclysmic events. I uncovered the evidence of at least 15 previous visitations of this dreadful scourge of the forces of cosmic nature upon our galaxy. For the best part of my 4 life spans I devoted myself to the means of avoiding the 16th coming. I had unearthed the nature of the force which regularly sweeps through the vastness of our universe with regular almost rhythmic precision leaving a cold calling card on each occasion. By peeling back layer upon layer of these enforced molecular changes, using our acquired knowledge of the sub atomic molecular make-up of our planet I found an antidote to this force of unstoppable and colossal magnitude. Like an anti-infestation programme, this force swept all living material before it purging land, sea and sky, of all living matter to then restart the process over and over. All this swept over our planet in the merest of time, no more than 1 second. Imagine the destruction of every living thing in so short a period of time! This time I thought to deny nature its course. With the scourge neutralised, our civilisation would continue unchecked to attain even higher levels of knowledge achievement and progress than at any other period of the planet's existence. It offered our race unimaginable opportunity, to extend beyond the limitations of a single lifetime span in global terms. Everybody eagerly accepted the truth of my findings and we hastened to complete our preparations. There is nothing like the prospect of extinction to stimulate the corporate and governing bodies into activity. Activity unparalleled, resulted in the creation of this station.

This was completed within my fifth life-span, which I had always considered to be my last by choice, and my dearest desire was to be left here within its structure in thanks at our ultimate deliverance. All went well until the chance discovery of an Earth-like planet, brought to our notice with the acceleration of the technology as we struggled with the project and its complexities. Far beyond our previous ranges of exploration, suddenly a new world offered rescue to the uneasy populations at large. This clamour grew into an irresistible demand for an alternative way, and many who had at first applauded the first option I offered them decided to seek a surer way.

A faction grew, gathering popularity for the focus to be switched to the new world and a new beginning. With a clever campaign promising riches, fresh hope, new opportunity, its leaders were able to manipulate the fears and superstitions of our people away from pure scientific fact to speculation and doubt as to the authenticity of our claims. It is not that difficult to understand the dilemma of their uneducated grasp of the realities and to see the benefits that the alternative choice offered. There were many who mistrusted science and the ability to produce the true solution whilst a tangible alternative was placed before them. Inevitably resources were redirected away from the prime solution to provide the means for escape and exodus to the new planet.

By the time the first evacuation was initiated, my project, depleted of funding and support all but came to a grinding halt. However with a few loyal staff and funded by my family alone, we completed the final stages of preparation at the very moment the last transports left Earth. They left unaware that the final pieces in the defence system were in place and ready. Alas they were not destined to be activated, at least not in my lifetime. So I elected to remain with my project in an ironic statement of defiance to my race, who were only too quick to abandon me here in their haste for self- preservation.

Unseen by any witness other than this lone satellite, the inevitable wave of destruction washed over tragic Earth in a repeat of Cosmic history, I have viewed its passing on the recorder since my reawakening. The effects were as terrible and heart rending as imagined, all the more poignant for the fact that at my fingertips lay the means of prevention.

And now, it is almost 200,000 years since those events and we stand on the threshold of this same threat yet again. Destiny it seems still intends for my contribution to be made. But there is much that you must still learn and understand if in fact we are to avoid the mistakes of those misguided people. Think of all that you have achieved in your known history, the material, the social, the physical triumphs. Then think of the continuity of those triumphs that you expect. Now consider those triumphs wiped out in the blink of an eye. I ask you to choose which destiny you would prefer. With wisdom we should see the dawning of the greatest phase of mankind's history yet to be.

My chronicles revealed that the destruction of my own time occurred on the 32nd day after evacuation, reshaping oceans and seas even the continents themselves , erasing all but the most microscopic of organisms as the remnants of our proud civilisation. Such a waste such a waste..... needless...."

Dhoran seemed to struggle for an instant as the enormity of his realisation of the losses almost overpowered his emotions.

"Scrolling through the later histories, I was astonished to find evidence of a manned flight from this satellite back to Earth, 50 years to the day from the destruction. I had believed that all of our people had fled, but it seems there were indeed some intrepid believers left at the end. Closer inspection of the records revealed that some of the cryogenic chambers had been manually over-ridden to release their occupants for such a mission. Whether they succeeded in their adventure I do not know for there have been many other destructions since that of my own time. I would like to think that they enjoyed a lifetime of happiness together. In some way yet to be understood, you are probably descendants of that line and perhaps even related to me. That at least gladdens my heart and gives our destiny new meaning.

It appears that we each evolved in our own times to a similar level of accomplishment, and indeed a high level of technological supremacy, give or take a few refinements. Time as ever conspires to play its tricks upon us and all that we are capable of learning leaves even more to be understood. At that point before we can acquire the new knowledge the destruction is upon us again. This time however fate has dealt us a fresh hand and we may yet determine a new course, our advances gifted to your generation will surely lead us into and beyond the next evolutionary step.

We have much more to prepare and we are so few for the task. We have opposition as before, this time however more aggressive and destructive than ever before. Even now as we speak Earth forces are gathering, preparing to destroy yet again that which it does not understand and that which it can only see as a threat. I sense your disbelief. There are 200 or more Earth ships approaching this facility, making preparations for a direct assault and attack. I understand them and am not angered, more sorrowed at their futility and ignorance.

Jasmine, I am sorry for your tragic loss. He was in many ways the architect of this unwelcome black side of man's greed and thirst for power, but he was not a bad man. Misguided perhaps and certainly misled by those he trusted.

His courage and foresight were true however, and he carried the hope of ultimately benefiting his fellow man. This will come as a surprise to you Mike. You have lately come to regret your haste in judging this man, but your suspicion and scepticism may yet prove useful. Jasmine, you have spoken at length of your knowledge of the activities in which your father was engaged, but there is still much left to reveal. Perhaps now is the appropriate moment to tell all of us about the faith placed in your father by the world government. Somewhere within the genes of every living creature, the memories and knowledge of this place exist. For the most they remain buried surfacing only as dreams and fantasy, but occasionally they surface in a very few, as visions and real goals to be realised. So it was with your father. He chose to share his vision with a very powerful and astute person in the form of your Earth President. This trust and faith led to the means by which his greatest dream was realised. Yes your father knew all along of this place and the power it holds. What he had not yet understood before he died was the purpose. He did know that the next destruction was to strike a mere 7 days from this day. So that you can know why both of your father's were prepared to die for their belief in the future of mankind, not just their mankind but future generations, I must tell you that they agreed on a course of action after their momentous discovery. Oh yes Mike, your father also knew of this place, visited it many times with Rick. Each knew that there was a common enemy in their midst, until recently they could not have guessed that Paul hungered for the power of discovery and recognition and the ultimate corruption of that power led directly to the sorry entanglement we now face. That you two remained as witness to his greed and folly seems to have been destined from the outset, and as such you have always represented a danger to a small man's consumption of greed.

For myself, I had decided that my life should end at this next destruction. During my reawakening I was cursing at myself for my vanity in wanting to continue this fruitless vigil with little purpose. Had we not met, that plan would have been realised. But in you I see the survival of my own family, and I am driven to new hope for our race.

My question now is simple. Do you trust me enough to forge our new future together?"

Mike sat unmoving for a few moments before looking first at Jack, then at Jasmine and finally returned his gaze to Dhoran.

"Tell us what we must do."

CHAPTER SEVENTEEN: COUNTER ATTACK

Whichever way he looked at the problem, the Commander faced serious concerns. Approaching the "object" directly activated a powerful force field which he had established from the probe data extended outwards from the newly exposed "face" of the Moon whenever a 2 mile zone was breached. Not that he was able to reconcile the structure before him with any image of his perception of serene Moon.

Pulsating regularly with blue, white and yellow light, the sheer scale of the construction vied with the awesome realisation of the engineering prowess of whoever or whatever had created it. Added to that was the frustration that with all the resources of Earth's finest scientific minds, they had failed to establish beyond doubt the nature and purpose of its being there at all. Was it a weapon, was it an alien artefact, a ship? Whatever the perception, Earth had responded with its usual response to the unknown -   force! Whether that was the correct response in this instance was not really his concern, He had his orders and those he could relate and react to in keeping with his long and distinguished career in the military.

Even so, he had to admit to a grudging admiration for

the creation of something this spectacular. This close up, the intricacy and symmetry left no doubt as to the superiority of its makers. For all of his admiration John Gregg was under no illusions of feeling in any way inferior or under direct threat from "bug eyed monsters" and the like. He was well aware that any signs of intelligent life on this side of the known galaxy had long ago been established as an impossibility. So what he was dealing with here amounted to a legacy, perhaps from time before known time. Far fetched and crazy as the idea sounded, looking at the vista before him, far fetched and crazy seemed quite appropriate just now!

Whoever had designed this monstrosity had obviously prepared well. That something this large had gone undetected for so long, and yet still be active was amazing in itself. Then the reality of the scale of it was beyond human comprehension. If this turned out to be a weapon, and there were no end of discussions and debates even on that issue, then there were other questions to be answered regarding power sources and purpose. If not a weapon then what other purpose might it serve? He guessed that his orders to mobilise his forces logically was the only sensible decision they could have made given the level of knowledge, or ignorance for that matter, of this threat. Even as he watched, the structure was still evolving and manifesting itself, In complex and intricate patterns the metallic looking surface material appeared to rise in towers of fluid-like appearance; detaching themselves from the surrounding darkness and spiralling towards a starkly defined central spike in the fashion of a self sprung wheel-like structure. The ends of these columns attached themselves with uncanny accuracy and precision at pre-selected points around the enormous central shaft. In the one hour he had been at the observation window, three more "spokes" had completed their cycle. As the process was completed the spokes energised and took up the pattern of pulsating lights that they had noticed on approach which only served to heighten the tension and menace of the device the closer Earthforce got to their objective.

Mobilised at short notice Earthforce Command had broken all records in reaching their destination, only to lose any advantage in the frustration of waiting for expert analysis to determine their next move. John , although a loyal soldier well experienced and mature despite his 28 years, was never happy in these situations. By nature an adventurer and, without being reckless, driven to action before thought, he had to fight an inner mental battle with himself for the sake of the troops under his command. His assault force numbered 30 battle-cruisers, 200 rapid assault ships and at least 1000 single fighters. For all of their awesome firepower, until he was given the green light, they sat here motionless and unable to take any kind of action. The force field they had encountered shut down all systems, including life support, in any vessel which breached the "exclusion zone". With the loss of 200 men and 2 derelict rapid assault craft so far he had little option but to accept these restraints on his Command until they worked out a way to eradicate them.

So for now, here they sat. Earth's finest, powerless in the face of unknown forces. 'There has to be a way through' he thought to himself and decided only he could find it. As the youngest ever Commander, he felt his responsibilities deeply. He held an inner pride within himself at his ability to motivate and inspire the multinational force under his wing. Despite a background devoid of any military heritage, John Gregg was a rare breed of man, a born leader. He was a gifted strategist and theorist with an uncanny degree of intuition, all of which he used to give himself an invisible advantage over his contemporaries. Time after time and test after test these abilities singled him out as uniquely suited to military service and disciplines. When coupled to his passion for the stars and his brilliant student successes, his progress through college, military academy and the ranks had been as meteoric and breathtaking as any space launch. His promotion through the ranks had been compelling to watch, getting him to his present posting in less time than it took most of his age group to graduate the college.

The price of that success he had already acknowledged. He was single and a confirmed loner. Sometimes this tended to isolate him from those around him, and he was often considered to be aloof and unapproachable. Only those who knew him well were aware of his sensitive nature and vulnerability when it came to personal relationships. Even then he trusted nobody. Nobody but Gabby anyway. Gabrielle Fortenay had always been able to see through the shell he wore as though it were transparent. He had felt comfortable and secure with her and shared with her all his inner feelings and fears. He had told her of his years of loneliness in foster care after the tragic loss of both of his parents in a mysterious accident on a tourist shuttle during the early years of lunar travel and exploration. They'd been having fun on a hard earned vacation trip leaving him in the care of his grandparents. The tragedy had broken them too and eventually they were unable to continue to care for him themselves. He often wondered if his fascination for the stars had its foundation in that loss. Sadly, Gabby was thousands of miles away on Earth, like the rest of the world watching his every move and decision with bated breath wondering what the outcome would be and if they would still be safe tomorrow. If he could have done, he would have talked over his fears and thoughts with her, trusting her completely without concern for his image or his pride,

She was the only honest person he had ever met he reflected as he looked at her picture on the desk. But she was not here and he turned to his favourite method of creating his next move. As he always did, he turned to humble paper and pencil and recorded his seemingly random thoughts as they flitted across his mind. Once he had performed that ritual, he moved into his meditation and shed the military mode in preference to his free spirit in the subconscious world of his imagination. Often during these journeys, his apparent random thoughts had crystallised into flawless strategy and logic. Having made sure that his first officer was aware of his plan, he moved towards that special state now. The crew knew his routine and he was confident he would not be disturbed for the next two hours. After a final glance at Gabby's picture, he strapped himself down to the comfortable padded bench and prepared for his journey.

He dismissed his minds eye picture of the fleet held at bay by an unseen force, and the thoughts of the threat his force raised against his native planet. He initiated the mind cleansing ritual his grandfather had taught him. Wordlessly he performed his mantra chant keeping his inner rhythm on a down-beat as he did so. He recognised the moment his inner mind lifted off onto the high path and soared like a bird on its current. This part of the journey was as familiar to him as his ship routine and he deliberately drove himself towards his favourite vantage point on the journey to his subconscious inner mind. This was always the start of the unscrambling of his thoughts and the laying down of the solutions he had sought in the past. This time he instinctively felt that he had a real fight on his hands as the atmosphere this time was tense and threatening. He could sense the unravelling of the random thoughts on his imaginary piece of paper and decided to throw in all he knew of the events leading up to this point, from the first stages of lunar exploration to colonisation and settlement right up the sequence of tragic events on the Moon that led him here. He was looking for a clue, a hook, something that linked all of these events together for whatever purpose. If he had that, he knew he would have his starting point. He gave himself completely to the process and began to soar like a bird over familiar terrain.

He recognised the view of a sun-kissed landscape of red sandstone buttes overlooking fertile green plains and valleys interlaced with the silver like threads of sparkling streams. This was his peaceful place, the clear blue sky unblemished with cloud, a golden sun beaming down and giving him warmth and strength as he hovered on one of the thermals. He enjoyed this place, likening it to the freedom he found whenever he was in space. Soon though, he began to experience a different sensation which gradually intruded upon his pleasure. Reluctantly he forced himself to turn towards the cause of the interruption. There was an intruder in his sky and he felt threatened by its presence. Shadow-like, the presence eluded his every attempt to reveal its nature. He chased it and tried to outmanoeuvre it but failed to catch any part of its essence. 'Time to get smart' he thought knowing instinctively that if he won this particular skirmish he would have the answers he sought. The flight became a battle of wits as he whirled and swooped and circled, trying to turn from stalked to stalker long enough to gain the knowledge. Finally he made the transition to the higher level of subconscious thought. Hyper quick and hyper sharp his focus turned and stared into the face of his stalker and then he just knew.

"Commander on the bridge"

The crew acknowledged him as he made for the com and took up his position at the console.

"As you were, Captain". John looked up at his 1st

Officer, eyes still swollen and darkened from a hasty return to his conscious state. "Here are your instructions for relay to the fleet. Ensure they are implemented to the letter in full and unaltered! When you have them at the ready, pipe me back up. You have the command."

"Yes Commander!" Without even glancing at the coded instructions, Pablo Harding acknowledged John's instructions and saw him off the bridge to his quarters before helping him to his bunk in a state of near collapse. Once back at the helm, he opened up the command programme making sure he understood the complex strategy by re-scrolling the campod display several times over. Acutely aware of the stakes, he settled down to implement the plan in full with the precision he knew was expected of him. In their situation and knowing the Commander as well as he did, Pablo knew they had only one chance to make the plan work. It never occurred to him to even question John's strategy such was his and the crew's faith in their Commander.

Sure that he understood the priorities and had them all correctly sequenced, Pablo initiated the first phase of signals to prepare and brief the fleet captains for their role in the plan. With some grim satisfaction he warmed to the task as he realised that it meant the end of their enforced inactivity. After seven days of preparations both he and the crew were raring to go. With such a vital task ahead of them the motivation was now doubled.

With absolute precision and attention to the smallest of details, Pablo did what he did best, strategy and planning in absolute detail every facet of the battle plan visualised in the draft plan. As routine he programmed three contingencies to every variable he came across until he was satisfied he could produce the desired end result without question. His quick mind and dextrous manipulation of the correlations within the matrix once entered in the strategy shunt, provided a very clear analysis of the attack plan. The simulation was showing 85% probability of success. 'Good enough' he swore silently to himself, totally committed to his role of ensuring the planned operation actually worked in their favour on demand.

"In position Commander." John acknowledged the last of the confirmations and then turned to face his deck officers.

"Let's do it!"

As one the formation of ships turned on an invisible axis until the sunlight flared off their surface wings giving the effect of a shining wedge shaped "V". On the moonward side they appeared as a black hole in the backdrop of stars. When alignment was complete, one ship broke away from the formation and stood off as if inspecting a parade.

John watched the effect of the formation on the Moon's surface, forwarding minute alterations to the fleet as it steadied and made preparations for the final manoeuvre. He noted the progress of the shadow created against the surface. Once he was satisfied he had tracked the passage accurately he rechecked the bearings of his own ship and began his final approach towards the surface. If he was right, they would have one point of opportunity, one opening which if missed would spoil any further attempts, the element of surprise would be gone and the initiative lost to whoever was orchestrating the defences down there.

Speeding out from under the shadow of the wing forming the fleet shield, John's ship, The Craven, made the transition from brilliant sunlight to darkness in the blink of an eye before homing in and centring up on the hub of the ethereal wheel forming ahead of them. So far so good, it appeared that the manoeuvre had fooled the defence system into accepting the fleet as a non-threat, the temperature indicator stayed anchored on the right side of comfortable.

The ship now angled her approach aiming for the trailing arm of one of the developing tentacles seeking to anchor itself at the hub. At this range now, not only could John discern the formation evolution in its spiralling transit across the Moon face, but it was also spreading downwards to meet the exposed metallic surface below the hub and out towards the solidifying rim beyond their narrowing field of vision. With only a few minutes remaining before they reached their objective, he knew they had used the decoy to its maximum as slowly at first the first indications of the warm up hit the ships outer skin and the temperature began to creep upwards again.

With some urgency now, John switched on the thermal seekers aiming for a point between the incoming trailing edge of the spoke and the hub itself. He was still not sure exactly what to look for as they got closer. With one eye very firmly on the temperature readings and the other on the rapidly approaching view of the surface, a hint of desperation began to creep into his commands as he voice activated the delicate close manoeuvres needed for a manual landing like this. Hotspots began to form on the schematic of the hull indicating the fine line he was drawing between landing and disintegration. Still seeking out a landing site, their worst fears were realised as the thermoalarm shrieked out its strident protest as the temperature soared dangerously unchecked and they all felt it even through the pressure suits.

"They're onto us Commander" Jake called out in alarm as his work station flared up in sparks and melted.

"Now or never then!" John gritted his teeth through the searing heat and discharged the grapple anchors away. The super powerful magnetic grabs should have hit the surface with a definitive thud. Instead John was surprised as they appeared to join with the material as though sinking into soft toffee. "That looks a little unstable" he understated.

"All EVA gear up and running now! Looks like we're going in on foot!"

As the assault team exited the ship, the fleet shield completed its task and veered away, casting a brilliant golden light on the attack site. His crack team were poised just above, what appeared to be, an over-large airlock. Jock the first Engineer was concentrating intensely on his compupad, periodically checking a light display emanating from the face of the wall to the left of the lock. He was attempting to match what appeared to be a light pattern being emitted at high frequency. Anxious seconds passed by as they waited, the reflected solar glare now beginning to challenge the integrity of their space suits. Little by little the comfort zone was being eroded and John felt justified in hurrying him on.

"Come on Jock! We're cooking out here!"

"I know commander, nearly there!"

It was a little unfair on Jock, he too was gradually turning a nice shade of lobster pink.

"Step on it man....!"

"We're in!" Jock almost bellowed as he keyed in the final elements to the code. Nothing happened

"Jock?"

Jock edged forward slowly on thrusters. Expecting to come up short against the door of the airlock , instead he touched down and promptly fell through what now appeared to be a liquid mass. On his lead the remaining 14 followed suit, weapons at the ready.

By the time John followed them through, he was experiencing an unpleasant and strident high pitched whine through his headset. As he turned around to face the airlock door, he thought he saw it ripple and then stabilise. Tentatively he reached out and touched it again. This time it was solid.

"Skipper, there's another door just like the last one up ahead. Shall we go through?"

"Affirmative, with full caution! Let's be ready for whatever lies on the other side. Check weapons!"

He knew it was an unnecessary order. This crew had to be perfect before John would even consider them for his own. Each man could be trusted with the command itself if necessary such was his trust in them. As they gathered at the second door, the high pitched whine began again. Guessing the significance now, three abreast they ran at the door weapons armed and at the ready. As if choreographed the 15 men fanned out into a standard but deadly formation and were met with silence. John scanned the corridors fanning out and away from them stopping short as a single black suited figure emerged from the corridor to his right. The weapon he held, unlike anything John had seen before was being held in an obviously passive stance.

"Commander Gregg! Would you please come with me and advise your men to stand down please!"

The voice although somewhat mechanical in nature was strangely familiar to him.

"Surrender now or face annihilation!"

As the figure in black spoke, the immediate area around them became softly but effectively illuminated, as if the rock itself were giving off a subdued light. As he surveyed the area, wherever he looked menacing ranks of black suited troops were poised weapons levelled and pointed in their direction. 'So much for the element of surprise' he thought to himself.

"I think not!" he replied as the lines of black first wavered and then blinked out leaving a force of just three figures holding them in check. "Good work Jock!"

Jock had had the presence of mind to check for life signs as soon as they entered the interior. As one of the original engineers involved in the Quorum technology, he had swiftly identified and eliminated the false threat with ease.

The odds were new very much in John's favour. He took the weapon from the being in front of him, noting with satisfaction that its companions had handed theirs over too.

"Now, *you* take me to your commander or whoever it is you report to. Who are you and what are you doing here?"

The black figure seemed to weigh him up for a moment, as if taking stock of the man, then with a brief nod to his companions, with deliberate slowness to avoid any misunderstandings, all three began to remove their black visors.

"It's good to see you again Gregg!"

John stepped back in surprise.

"Rick! What the hell are you doing here?"

"Plenty of time for explanations later Commander. We need your help and firepower badly. But first we have got to work out exactly how to get your force in. Come with me, we've secured an area just a short distance from here. I can brief you and your advance team better from there. We've got big problems up here, and we're sure glad your party made it through OK.

By the time Rick had completed the full story, John was already working and visualising his attack plan. One thing that he now knew for certain, Time was a luxury they did not have!

CHAPTER EIGHTEEN: HOMEWARD BOUND

Bhodran settled uneasily into the gravcouch. His previous memory of space travel ended at the point at which he entered the cryotank assigned to him at Exodus. Whilst his faith in the skills and abilities of the Scientist Class remained rock steady, nevertheless this new concept of travel "faster then light" made him nervous. At first moving around the ship had been a novelty and a form of light relief in stark contrast to the unfamiliar aggressive nature of the adventure in which he now found himself involved. On what was in essence a stripped down transporter, hastily converted into a carrier of death and destruction, in very short order he had become intimately acquainted with every centimetre of unpainted metal, every rivet and every nut and bolt of her structure. This return trip was going to take a mere fraction of the time it had taken to travel the same distance at Exodus, the blink of an eye compared to a long night's sleep. Even so with no assigned duties on board to take care of during the long hours of flight, he was left to his own devices most of the time. Not that he didn't have *anything* to do of course. His official title was Cultural Attaché. Effectively this meant he had been given free reign to prepare for the aftermath of what by all accounts was to be a swift, bloody and decisive attack on the inhabitants of their former home world Terrania. Despite the disadvantages of facing an unknown enemy, quite possibly an entirely different species to their own, the Strategists had argued that they had the advantage of fighting on familiar territory, and that they had the element of surprise in their favour. Knowing nothing of military strategy, Bhodran could only give them the benefit of doubt. Despite this, he had a deep feeling of foreboding at what he perceived to be an ill advised and unnecessary attack. He had expressed these feelings freely and often but to no avail. Vengeance and retaliation ruled the Council's decision to choose the Military option. He felt that he was regarded as an afterthought almost, a token conciliatory presence after the event.

With a deep sigh, he returned to his self-designated task in hand. He knew he should have felt gratitude and pride in these labours. Instead he felt as though he was being humoured and kept busy so that the crew and officers would not have to deal with his insistent pleas for a rethink of their plans. After all he was but a mere academic theologian. What did he know of war and battles?

Once again he scrutinised the revered casket on his workstation bench from every angle, even though he knew it intimately by now. A hexagonal hardened alloy casing inlaid with a mixture of bronze and brass banding, it was designed to split horizontally into a series of detachable compartments. Each compartment held a disk of pliable but unbreakable metal-like material. There were 15 compartments altogether. Of the 15 he had so far only managed to fully translate 5 of the enigmatic disks with the aid of an ancient but effective laser reader and decoding machine. Most of the problems in disseminating the information lay in the condition of the disks themselves. Despite the precision engineering of their containers, corruption had spoiled the once mirror perfect surfaces, leaving large areas of information illegible and lost forever. This meant that accurate translation and understanding of the contents was compromised with the addition of his own deductions and laws of probability to fill in the gaps, not to mention the element of "guesswork" also involved.

It was this obvious fallibility in the resulting translations, which lead the "hawks" in the Command to dismiss his entreaties to reconsider their stance on the basis that unsupported "guesswork" was not enough. The facts stood, their world had been taken from them, and they now had the means to retake what was formerly theirs. They would not move from this course of action unless he had irrefutable evidence to convince them otherwise. They would no longer tolerate the pseudo-existence of Novadom when there was the tantalizing prospect of the prize of a normal life to be won. As such he had no argument but to return to his studies in the hope that he could make the connection, find the thread that eluded him and his predecessors in discovering their long lost history in all its glory.

Methodical as ever, he now laid the 15 disks in order of their presentation in a long line in front of him on the makeshift desk of his cabin companion's bunk. 'If only there were some way to speed up the translations" he mused to himself. Strange that the script was so closely related to their own yet predating it by at least one millennia, almost as though whoever had written it was deliberately concealing something, and if so why? For some reason, one of the disks caught his eye, number 11 in the sequence. The harsh lighting of the cabin unfiltered above the bunk made that particular disk appear as though it was of a different texture from the others, but from a certain angle only. An elusive symbol seemed to have been etched on the face of the disk that he had never noticed before. Instinctively he knew this had to be a further clue to the puzzle, but what was it trying to tell him?

Captain Storphan hailed the fleet. "All ships, standby for instructions! All stop!"

As a former veteran of Terrania's mighty navy of off world ships, Storphan commanded the respect of the entire fleet under his command, from lowly cabin boy to the Admiralty, he was acknowledged as a master tactician and a superb motivator of men. Before the Exodus, he had been hailed as the Saviour of the Race in the simulated games of war at the Academy in Renso. As a young and energetic 29 year old, his appointment to Fleet Captain, whilst swift, on this occasion was borne of necessity. Of the missing 1000 ships which had carried the majority of Fleet Command, his had been the only surviving ship with ratings of any level to come through to Novadon. Now he felt powerful and purposeful, ready for the coming action. He also felt that he had a lot to prove both to himself and those under his command, knowing only too well that his recent battle experience was very thin.

As one, aided by the mastercomm on board the flagship Petrovan, all 100-assault ships hove to. From his observation port, Storphan nodded in satisfaction at the sight of all ships intact and in formation after their first "jump". He had feared that in the haste of preparation and departure, safety and security could have been compromised. Whilst the functional square formed transporter conversions would win few design awards for style and elegance, they were formidable fighting craft nonetheless. Each sported a bank of 10 theurion cannon forward, each one capable of destroying a minor asteroid at long range, plus a row of spatamonic torpedo launchers spaced evenly around the flanks of each ship. For good measure they had added fluxwhip stingers in the tail sections. These trailed the ships at 100 metres. He imagined them metaphorically flexing in the solar winds, their lethal charges of 1 million eonates capable of disabling any hostile craft within 10 km with a single discharge.

As he entered the Ready Room, a converted dorm, he glanced over the assembled ranks of officers and men, those standing at attention on the Petrovan, and those he could see on the overhead monitor displays. All, he knew, were primed and ready for the task ahead of them, whatever that entailed. Though none of them had ever been called upon to take territory on this scale by force before, the endless simulations he had them endure during their flight so far, had them all honed to a fine edge of preparedness. Disable, Confuse and Penetrate were at the heart of their tactics, each Commander was designated a detailed support strategy to follow through their commando strike. Their prize would be the old homeworld, Terrania! It had to be enough, simple and daring. He knew each man involved individually, and instinctively knew their courage and faith would not be wanting in any respect.

"All ships linked up and standing by Captain!"

Storphan acknowledged his number one Grolvan with a nod as he turned to face the newly formed Terranian Assault Force.

"We have arrived at the first of 10 jump points between here and Terrania. These stops are necessary for the focusing of the directional jump indicators. After so many years, it is wise to check the accuracy of our ancient charts as given in the sacred scriptures. We all know the prime objective, just as we know that the task we have set ourselves will be difficult, bloody, but righteous! At each of these jump stops we must calibrate our position, our weapons and our focus in final readiness for our glorious crusade to retake our birthright, Terrania. Only when we reach the 6th jump will we finally have the first sight of our world. Only then will we be able to see the resistance we face. WILL WE FALTER?"

"NO!"

"WILL WE PREVAIL?"

"YES!"

"WILL WE CONQUER!"

"YES!"

The responses came like a single laser shot. Satisfied that their fervour and enthusiasm were at full effect, Storphan left the briefing room to the tacticians and made for the bridge.

"How long before we are underway?"

"Two hours Sir!"

"Very well Grolvan, Carry on!"

"Commander! Wait! I have it! I have it all Sir!"

Storphan wheeled around angrily. "Who dares to invade my bridge at this crucial time? Oh it's you Bhodran! What do you want?" he added testily, angered at such a breach in his security. The Admiral's doom laden aide was the last thing he wanted right now. "Who let this man on my bridge?" he roared at his officers

"I did Captain, I'm sorry." The Admiral stepped through the door to stand behind Bhodran. Storphan was caught unaware that the Admiral was present. He made a mental note to quiz his first officer.

"Attention all hands!"

"Stand easy Captain. Bhodran I believe is about to stop us all from making the gravest of errors. I insist that you hear what he has to tell us before we proceed. This will take no more than 2 hours, after which we must decide on our Attack Plan with enlightened minds."

CHAPTER NINETEEN: AGAINST THE FLOW

Jack frowned at the data streaming across his access screen, glancing above, his eyes darting from monitor to monitor.

"Looks like we've got company!" he announced to the room in general. "The Earth force managed to land an advance assault team in sector 13 by the looks of it."

"They will not be any cause of concern to us down there" Dhoran assured him. "Nor will their efforts have the slightest impact upon our preparations here. They seem to have joined forces with another group of 3 or 4 people of whom I was not aware. Now that is a revelation!"

Dhoran seemed genuinely surprised. He did not like the idea of uninvited and unknown guests at such a critical time. He thought he had covered and accounted for all the activities on the station, even down to the many additional numbers of people in sector 91 who had materialised on his count only recently. Yet another breach in his security! And now this determined group of armed troops had managed to enter his system with apparent impunity. He made a mental note to review all his security facilities. "Mike, we are almost ready. There are but two hours remaining before the event. Are your preparations complete?"

"Yes Dhoran, even though half of what we've loaded up

doesn't make much sense to me, we have completed all of the instructions given so far. You agree to the final sequence run down?"

"Yes Mike. It is essential that all input through the initiator tripads be activated on each of the 12 prime control pads at precisely the same moment. There is no room for even the slightest delay otherwise the Drangue Beam will fail to energise at all! The lack of personnel does not help us in this fact but I am sure the Quorums will make for good substitutes. You have programmed them well. We have, as you say, done all that we could be expected to do. The rest is fate. Mankind will either applaud you and thank you for their deliverance or, they will simply no longer exist. For me you must understand, this is the vindication of five of my lifetime's work. This puts to the test the theories and calculations and above all my own beliefs in the elevation of mankind to his most exalted place and the release of unknown and unlimited potential. Come now, enough talk. We must prepare!"

Jasmine appeared casually from the galley, and handed steaming cups of what passed close enough to coffee to Mike and Jack before taking her place in the master chair. During their long hours of the knowledge assimilation, she had proven to be the most suited to the delicate task of fine tuning the calculations of the myriad of complex instruments they had been introduced to during their intense forced learning sessions. Dhoran had thoroughly briefed them all on the need for total accuracy in all of their manoeuvres, but it fell to Jasmine alone to ensure that the aim was beyond error. Within herself, despite her calm relaxed exterior, she was stretched to the limits of endurance. Every nerve, every muscle, every fibre of her being was as taut as a manogata string bow. Her emotional state was well dampened thanks to Dhorans manipulations at the control sessions. Even so they were all aware of her delicate state and treated her accordingly, mindful of the gigantic responsibility the situation now demanded of her.

One final time, Dhoran took them through their practised routine, noting with satisfaction the ease now at which the 'Newlings' as he'd decided to call them, performed a flawless run through of the synchronised action he required. No need to remind them of the cosmic significance of their actions, their instincts now showed them all the ramifications of success and failure. They would not fail easily. Any doubts he might have had of their ability to absorb and learn all there was to know about his world, his theories and his work were gone. It had still taken a giant leap of faith for them to trust him enough to subject themselves so readily to his cause. For their part, they were unanimous in their resolute support for him and his efforts to save their world, his own long since beyond redemption. Theirs was the thrill of realisation, not only in the incredible detail of information they had absorbed, but an inner pride at the uniqueness in holding the fate of the world and all of its inhabitants at their fingertips. The prizes of success were obvious, super advances and a future unfettered like any other before. They were young enough to benefit from this success and would become willing disciples for generations to follow.

As the time advanced towards their moment of truth, their courage showed on each of their faces as, with no fear or hesitation, they each began the final alignments and adjustments to their control panels and issued their instructions to the Quorum teams. At the prearranged signal from Dhoran the first stage protocols and procedures were initiated.

Paul seethed with frustration as bank after bank of controls refused to allow him access to any of the main functions. He was well aware that a higher intelligence was at work somewhere, but refused to acknowledge the fact. All but essential life support systems were frozen. He refused to give up yet

"Let's go hunting!" he sneered as he turned away from the immobile displays and turned towards his companions. "I know places within this pile of junk nobody else does. They tried to shut me down, well they're going to wish they hadn't even thought about it by the time we're finished!"

His hand picked elite squad made final preparations as they checked their weapons and then checked those of their comrades. With a precision that would be the pride of the Earthforce Commando themselves, they formed up and made double time to the waiting transports.

"Paul. How are we going to get at them through the tunnels?"

Matt was a small but powerfully muscular man and one of Paul's staunchest supporters and protectors. He had loyally followed him since he could legally join up and relentlessly followed Paul's exploits as an explorer and businessman of steel with relish. At 21 he had abandoned the Earthforce battalion in favour of a high command within Paul's notoriously brutal security guard. There, his persistence and sheer bravado had caught Paul's eye and he quickly became an established, trusted and dependable soldier to the cause. If there was dirty work to be done, without hesitation Matt was the man. Here, the question was put not out of fear rather than curiosity and the mark of a strategic brain at work.

"All the tunnels are fluxing now which puts them on a never ending loop doesn't it?

"My dear fellow, they have forgotten or simply don't realise that in three years of exploration and surveying this turd of a planet, I have found a simple weakness. The maintenance tunnels are the exception to the rule. They have to remain constants. As such they give access to most of the sectors, but more importantly, they lead straight to the nerve centre which is where we want to be."

Paul took the controls himself, his large fingers dancing delicately over the keypad as he entered a sequence of commands and them sat back in anticipation of the ride to come. The craft's acceleration pushed them deeply into the padded seats as they both buckled themselves firmly into place expecting the ride to be smooth as normal. This time however the ride was not as expected. Neither Paul nor his cohort had anticipated that others would have foreseen this eventuality and laid traps to hold them back. Each junction within the network met them with a resistance charge, even the automatic dampening devices began to act intermittently. The net effect was the sensation of being hurtled down a never-ending black tube at high speed with constant spine jarring vibrations punctuated with painful concussions at every junction.

He had anticipated their transit time at 15 minutes but even so Paul knew they would not survive the punishing ride intact. He quickly ordered his team to prime the wristjectors to 15 minutes and activate. He did not care about their discomfort so much, but wanted them battle-ready at their arrival point. He gave the signal and as one the team slumped unconscious in their harnesses, all but Paul himself. Single minded now in his determination to secure his ultimate objective, he endured every sickening jolt and bump as though he was immune to their effects. He began to visualise their destination now and plotted out the inevitable fire-fight that would announce their arrival. As he closed his eyes in concentration, a feeling of dread swept over him momentarily. He imagined in stark reality a surreal image of the distorted face of his former "partner" mockingly laughing at him, pointing an accusing finger at him, warning him? From the grasp of death? Surely.......!

"Commander, we have incoming!" called out the trooper.

John turned on his heel taking in the final preparations. "What direction and how many?"

"Hard to say for sure sir, these readings are as confused as hell! Could be three transports, could be just the one. However many it is, they don't plan on using the brakes! We're looking at between 10 and 60 strong!"

Satisfied that his defences were as effective as they could be, John switched his thoughts to the strategy beyond this skirmish. If they could get to the command centre despite the complex maze of fluid tubes of the internal transport system, then there had to be some way of using that to his advantage. Rick joined him as he stood his ground watching for the point of attack.

"If that is Paul, he knows that system better than anybody else. Assume nothing and expect the assault to be with total force!"

"Thanks for the advice sir, my men are the best there is. With your help and expertise I think we have the upper hand. Central command briefed me fully on your involvement with this project from its conception. Your insight has already provided me with the tactical advantage we need. This fight is just for openers. You can anticipate much more to come. What I haven't fully appreciated is why this project has been so hush-hush. Until my briefing on the assault, even I was not aware that this satellite was anything but good old lunar "moon". We all knew there has been exploration and surveying as an ongoing commercial operation up here, but nothing on this scale. This is out of all proportion to what we know or think we know has been going on up here."

"John, if I told you, you just wouldn't believe me!"

"Try me, but make it fast. I'd like to know exactly what it is we are going to be fighting for in the next few minutes!"

"It'll take much longer than a couple of minutes, but suffice it to say that what it all comes down to is the survival of mankind. We have uncovered covert operations on Earth of a faction or factions that have contacted influences beyond the boundaries of the known universe........wait, wait hear me out! These factions have somehow forged an alliance, we don't know how, with these outside forces. We believe the alliance threatens Earth and its peoples for control and supremacy in the aftermath of the event."

"What event, what are you talking about Rick, this makes no sense!"

"No time John, here they come!"

Mike glanced anxiously at Jasmine. Six hours without a break was not good. She glanced back at him, seemed to read his thoughts and smiled.

"I'm fine, really. Don't worry!"

He grinned back and nodded. His own assignment was just as demanding. He turned his mind back to the task before him. Unfamiliar as he was with the technology, there was at least some synergy with his own discipline in astro-engineering, which he could relate to his task. He, Jasmine and Jack were all working towards the key point of total synchronisation of their efforts at the keyboards that demanded a split second timing they had never imagined they could achieve until their recent "schooling" at the hands of Dhoran. Even after the intensive training and practice runs which brought them to within micro-seconds of perfection, he still had doubts about his abilities, and imagined that both the others felt the same. The enormity of the mission facing them seemed like a dream, unreal, a game perhaps, but not so. He understood with stark clarity the impending threat to fragile Earth,and the unthinkable consequences should they fail. In the end, it all came down to these few people in this place at this time.

Dhoran broke his train of thought "Mike, I would like you to witness this with me. If proof were needed as to the necessity of our task to save the future of the people of planet Earth, then this is as close as we can make it so. Come."

Mike followed him to the enclave. One wall of the cell was illuminated with an image of the Earth and the Moon in their familiar guise and relationship. Beyond them both in the void of black space the simulation showed what looked like an angry storm filling the blackness with a swirling threatening mass of coloured mists advancing rapidly upon the two globes.

"From the archives recorded since my era, these images are a composite approximation of the effect of the "Event". The storm as it approaches, unlike this visualisation, is invisible and arrives unannounced. When it leaves, it leaves no witnesses. Watch!"

As they watched the simulation, the edge of the storm reached the atmosphere. In a blinding white blue flash in seconds the entire surface of Earth seemed to dissolve in a mass of dust and steam. When the glow faded again, the aftermath of its passage was clear to see. Where before the familiar blue and white marble dominated the blackness of space, in its place was a shrivelled dull grey ugly planet devoid of life and vitality.

"This has happened many times before even my birth, and many times since. The Earth has amazing powers of recovery. See how already she covers herself in a misty shroud as she begins the long road to recovery. Yes she will recover her former glory but to lose so much when we can disrupt this needless cycle of destruction, that has always been my dream. We now, the four of us, can realise that dream and begin a new chapter, a new beginning in the future history of mankind."

Dhoran seemed to be lost in his dreams for a few seconds, then recovered himself and advanced the image to show how their preparations would take effect if they succeeded this time.

Mike's throat felt as though it were gripped in a vice being closed relentlessly. He felt like screaming out, but no sound would come. All those lives, those people, the futility of Man's existence and struggles to grow, all for nothing! He could not swallow as he tried to comprehend the scale of the devastation in real terms. Their entire multi-coloured, multi-faceted civilisation gone --- just like that! Dhoran nodded as if comprehending the agony of the younger man's thoughts. He noted the changing expression from horror to resolution to determination.

"You're ready!" he said simply. "We have barely 15 minutes remaining. Please now, resume your station."

Mike resumed his position at the master console. He looked over the massed ranks of the Quorum teams behind him at the banks of secondary consoles. His eyes returned to the monitor in front of him. In a parody of the scene enacted on Dhoran's simulation, Earth and the now modified "Moon" showed against the blackness in real-time. The computer enhanced and simulated the advance of the threat in a series of green grid lines with an uneven leading edge, moving inextricably but perceptibly towards the suspended orbs.

He glanced over at Jasmine again, oddly amused at the sight of her multiple images, and then at Jack. Jack was mesmerised at his Quorum team, the "Narcissus" syndrome they called it. "Jack! Get a grip on it!" he growled. "This is for real remember!"

Jack jumped at the terse command. He had never gone through the Quorum training process before and quite apart from the novelty factor, he was unprepared for the exhilaration of sheer power he was feeling. The jolt was just what he needed as sanity returned and instinctively he shared the arrival of the moment of truth with his two companions. Smiling, he formed a thumbs up sign in compliance with Mike's implied command and turned frowning into his customary concentration mode.

"OK guys, let's begin the spiral into countdown, on my mark, three seconds from now – 2 – 1."

As one they threw their respective initiators. The sequencing confirmation lit up the master screen with a satisfying if indiscernible hum. Next Mike kicked in Phase 2 selector, followed with precise timing by Jack and Jasmine with Phase 3 and 4. "Perfect!" he murmured to himself. 'Now for the real fun!' he thought. At this point, the Quorum teams were programmed to initiate a series of complex and intricate instructions through the massed banks of computers. When they had completed that part of the task, the point of no return had been reached. Final countdown was almost an anti-climax, but concentration was an almost tangible feeling in the room. Working as a single entity, each of them bent to their own task, trusting each other and each other's teams to follow the drilled sequences with flawless competence. Looking up at Dhoran at the final point of initiation all four of them released the final coded instructions to the great machine and then waited

CHAPTER TWENTY: ENDINGS

The first attack came from an unexpected angle. Almost as if in slow motion, a speeding transport emerged from the ceiling 60 feet above them, momentarily diverting the Earthforce troops. They quickly recovered to meet this intrusion and stood fast ready for the expected onslaught. The carriages of the now harmless and crushed transport settled into a heap of splintered carbon and metal well away from the entrenched forces.

Mindful of the earlier Quorum firefight, John had deployed a bank of disrupters along their flanks and front-line positions. He wanted only solid targets in his sight this time.

An unnatural stillness and quiet descended upon the chamber as it quickly cleared of smoke and dust. Alert and eager now, they watched and waited for whatever was to come. They did not have too long to wait,

The first black-suited figures emerged from the wall of rock directly ahead of their positions. Four abreast they appeared to stumble forward in confusion and uncertainty, as if propelled forward from behind. They were met by an uncompromising stream of laser fire. The body count was just too fast.

"Cease fire! Cease fire!" John's urgent command stilled

the action almost immediately. Something was badly wrong here. These were not the fighting men they had expected. With an audible click, the fluid wall sealed itself off. It was quiet once again.

"Colin, go check out those casualties!" Under the watchful cover of the Earthforce team, Colin quickly reached the forward position where the bodies lay and knelt beside one of the fallen figures. Gingerly he pulled off the black visor. He was momentarily stunned to find himself looking into the dead features of an old woman of 60 or 70 years of age. He quickly recovered his composure, cursing at his involuntary feeling of revulsion before turning to check a few other fallen "enemy". This time he checked under the uniforms and discovered in each case the insignia of the Lunar Development Corporation.

"Civilians Sir! Goddamned civilians used as decoys!" Visibly affected, his choking words conveyed his feelings of utter contempt and revulsion for this blatant and inhuman treatment of innocent lives.

This was totally unexpected. John wondered where they could have come from. They were lunar workers but from where? The inhabitants of Lunar One had all perished hadn't they? A nagging suspicion was prodding at him from his subconscious. There had been no bodies left behind, they had all floated off into space......... unless?

Before he could develop the thought any further, the wall to their right exploded in a blinding flash of light and in the confined space of the chamber the percussion of the explosion was greatly amplified. This was without doubt the main event of the day.

"Back to position Col! Everybody, make sure your targets are weapon viable before you shoot. Stay alert! Fire at will!"

They all three looked at each other in expectation, of what exactly they weren't sure, and then turned to Dhoran.

"Did we do it?" asked Mike

Dhoran allowed himself a rare smile.

"See for yourselves my friends!" as he indicated the monitors.

As they followed his extended arm, they felt a thrill as the view, obviously from their vantage point in space framed the brilliant blue and white marbled ball of Earth starkly clear against the black backdrop filled with what seemed to be a sea of sparkling specks of light.

"Total success! We did it for sure!"

Lost in his own thoughts, Dhoran was only vaguely aware of the screams and shouts of jubilation as the Newlings celebrated their survival and the survival of their kind. He was already deep in troubled thought as he alone knew that there was a further threat to overcome.

Paul could sense that he was not going to win this skirmish. The force he was up against were well prepared and well trained, probably Earthforce Elite. His decoy option had faltered almost before it was initiated; whoever led the opposing troops was dangerously fast and astute. There had simply not been enough time to draw their fire so he could exploit any weaknesses he found there. All he had succeeded in doing was stirring up the hornet's nest, they were madder than hell now, and they would not accept the civilian casualties lightly. He began preparations for a swift exit. He would still have the element of surprise as long as he held the tunnels. Checking his hand held statpad he realised he had lost control of yet another section of the tunnel complex to his enemy, the one that would lead them to the discovery of the crynochambers where the remainder of the Lunar base hostages were being held in stasis. Well so be it, they had served their purpose now, he could afford to lose them. No, more important was the fact that time itself was rapidly running out and against him. If he didn't act soon, his initiative would be lost and the grand prize lost! The forthcoming Event was imminent. It had to be now or it would be too late!

He relayed a rapid string of instructions through Matt, ordering the men to fan out and advance using the cover of their mobile deflectors. He watched as his lieutenant personally relayed the instructions by hand before laying on a devastating barrage of laser cannon fire in the direction of the Earthforce positions.

He lost a few seconds dodging determined return fire before gaining the relative safety of a fluid doorway. Here he quickly checked over his personal transport. This was his own personal vehicle and differed from the general transports in every aspect. Beautifully machined and finished it was a sleek purposeful looking device, built for speed and comfort. This he regarded as his last chance to wrest control from the Earthmen. He had no choice but to succeed. It could not be too late. As he slipped into the contoured personally tailored seat, he casually finalised inputting the co-ordinates of his destination and activated the viewscreen. Pity about Matt, he mused, he was a good man. Engaging the motors, he settled in for yet another uncomfortable ride. The perspex cover slid closed over his head.

"Mike, Jasmine, Jack," beamed Dhoran. "You have fulfilled my lifelong's ambitions. You are without any doubt heroes and saviours of your race. You will soon be acclaimed as such and rewarded no doubt beyond your wildest dreams." He paused as if gathering himself for one of his dramatic revelations. "Over these eventful days, I have come to look upon you as both my friends and my family." Jack began to squirm with embarrassment but quietened as if he could sense Jasmine's displeasure. "You already know much of the events which have brought us to this moment, but before we go further, there are other aspects to this that you must be made aware of.

Jasmine, when your father and his team discovered this complex, they unwittingly set off a sequence of events which, but for our timely interventions, may yet have dire consequences far beyond the mere salvation and deliverance of your people and planet. Without knowing it they have activated within this complex, not merely the benign purpose for which it was built, awakening within it not only myself, but also awoken forces which might yet threaten Earth and its peoples."

Mike, puzzled by Dhoran's hesitancy and uncertain stance asked a seemingly obvious question.

"Why go to the trouble of saving the planet, only to threaten it again?"

Before Dhoran could address this question, Jasmine called them over to one of the monitors.

"Dhoran, everyone, come and take a look at this!"

On the monitor they had a clear picture of the action going on in the outer chamber as the firefight began to die down into sporadic sniping.

"Ah yes," said Dhoran, "the Earthforce Invasion. It looks as though the position is all but taken in Earthforce's favour."

As he spoke, the struggling remnants of Paul's troops realising the futility of their situation surrendered their arms to the Earth troop.

Jasmine paled visibly, transfixed by one of the Earthforce troopers walking purposefully towards the monitor. He gave a thumbs up sign as he removed his helmet. She paled visibly as she stared into Rick's face, smiling at them in triumph.

John quickly rounded up the remainder of the opposing

force, relieving them of their weapons and securing their capture with plascuffs to wrists and ankles before herding them unceremoniously towards the newly revealed boarding platform. They had proven no match for his elite group once deserted by their leader.

With horror and sadness, he turned his attentions to the score or so of downed civilian casualties. That somebody could so callously and cold-heartedly consider the expenditure of innocent lives with such a despicable deception beggared belief. He mentally joined a growing club of people determined to end the bloody excesses of this inhumane madman Paul Gregot. Rick joined him briefly, visibly affected by the sight of the pointless savagery. He was all the more affected because he personally recognised some of the victims from the survivors from Lunar One settlement. Rescued from the destruction of the base, their fate was to meet a tragic destiny here on a battlefield instead at the hands of his former ally and trusted friend Paul Gregot.

"It's time we nailed this bastard for good John!" he spat the words out now, struggling within himself to suppress the anger and anguish he felt at the heartless murder and carnage lying at his feet. In truth he felt in part responsible. Normally an astute judge of character, he felt very keenly that his had been the decision of bringing Paul into the Corporation in the first place. This enigmatic scheming butcher had ridiculed his elaborate screening process and betrayed him personally, and *that* he would not let that pass easily.

Paul had come to his attention a few years before the heady days of the colonisation programme. He had presented himself at the company HQ unannounced, managing to charm his way through, not only the reception security screening process, but also through a three tier deliberate stalling mechanism. Not only that but he had even managed to forge an alliance with his loyal secretary to the extent that he had been ushered into Rick's inner sanctum for an unheard of unscheduled interview. At the time he had admired the man's tenacity and ingenuity, judging him to be both resourceful and resilient, rare qualities he could usefully employ.

Since that first encounter, and after an exhaustive and elaborate background investigation, normal corporation procedure, the overwhelming result was one of admiration and satisfaction. Here stood a determined, accomplished, well prepared individual who had doggedly pursued his goal to work for the man he had pinpointed as his target and would-be mentor/ partner designate. Without doubt he possessed all the credentials and qualities he demanded of a personal aide. From the first interview to the last, Rick had warmed to the man and his attitude towards business and life in general, seeing in him a mirror image of himself. So much so that it seemed that in Paul's company, he did not need to put on his customary aloofness and distant charm offensives. He really liked him! After brief consultations with his partner Tom, he had personally foreshortened the normal protocols of induction to get him on board and functioning in half the normal 3 months. For a solid three years Paul diligently applied himself to become an effective understudy to his master. Not only that but to the annoyance and frustration of practically everyone else in the organisation who stood outside of Rick's inner circle, they had become good friends both in and outside of work. Naively and only admitting it to himself, he had been flattered and his ego boosted by the seemingly never-ending devotion of this one man to making his business life as seamless and smooth running as possible.

Only here on the Moon had it become clear that there had been an elaborate and comprehensive strategy to create an undetectable smoke screen, a facade exclusively for his benefit. It was to become a means to an end for the unravelling puzzle before them, only now becoming clearer with each twist and turn of events as they were happening. Rick had begun to suspect all was not as it appeared when the "discoveries" they were making seemed too convenient and easily uncovered. As each new clue of the lunar sub-surface complex was revealed, Paul's reaction had been subdued and calm, no sense of wonderment or disbelief had ever registered with him. Considering the nature of the incredible edifice they had uncovered together, his reaction of nonchalance had disturbed him a great deal, instinctively he took care not to voice his doubts to Paul himself. His concerns grew so strongly that he scheduled a special security council with the Earth president and his security Chief Adviser outside of the one's he routinely attended with Paul at his side. He had voiced his fears and observations that their discovery, so far held covertly away from the public domain until they understood its ramifications in greater detail. They all agreed that the possibility of a sinister infiltration of the facility was real. None of them could guess at its purpose, so the decision made was to monitor Paul's every move and report back. Rick felt somewhat relieved that his would not be the only "eyes and ears" so to speak keeping the project on track.

Eventually it had all come to a head that fateful evening in his study when the true nature of the beast had finally revealed itself in his "assassination". Thanks to Tom's ingenuity in the legacy of an experimental branch of the Quorum project, a realistic "victim" had been generated to provide a convincing subterfuge to throw Paul off guard. The process itself was similar to the Quorum team application, but Tom had found that by intensifying and concentrating the diffused elements within the containment tank for relatively short periods, the "hard-body" effect had been made possible, unstable as it was. Not only had Paul been totally convinced that he had murdered Rick, but if it hadn't been his own idea, he himself would have believed a real murder had in fact taken place. It had certainly convinced Jasmine when she had chanced upon the aftermath. He hadn't counted on that, but could do nothing to protect her from the inevitable anguish she would suffer. If she were recaptured he could not risk the truth falling into Paul's hands. This way he had kept the element of surprise, once the deed itself was done. That moment had unlocked more mysteries at a stroke than any of the enigmas they had encountered whilst working together over the last 8 years or so. Tom's murder was now so obvious, as was his murderer. That brought home another failing in him. Due to his arrogance and flippant dismissal of the accusations levelled at him by amongst others Tom's son, his son-in-law, Mike a heinous crime had so far gone unpunished. He should have done more to protect Tom, taken the fears seriously, anticipated the assassination perhaps. The fact that he had alienated Mike hurt him badly now, that and the fact that in so doing he had precipitated the split between Mike and Jasmine. So clear now with hindsight. There would come a reckoning, and soon, he determined to himself and revenge would be oh so sweet and slow! He would personally see to that!

Rick looked back at John, the President's personal choice of Commander for this mission. 'A good choice' he thought. He and the rest of his men were clearing away the remains of the wrecked diversionary transport and securing the area for the influx of troopers to disembark from the fleet now standing down from the immediate threat of battle. Communications had now been re-established, all hostile activity from the satellite over. John had just finished sending his condensed report to the Fleet Commander as Rick walked over.

"Strange moves Rick," he said, "seems like the purpose

of this lump of rock, moon, whatever it is turned out to be "friendly" after all! Have you seen the pictures yet? Look at this!"

John replayed the vidreport he'd downloaded from the Comship. The transmission showed a hasty realignment of the ship's camera towards Earth. One minute the serene blue, green and white globe was as normal. Next the entire globe was sheathed in what seemed to be an intense beam of white light emanating from the position of the Lunar device. It appeared as an expanding cone of "white noise" intensely packed pulses of light placing itself as a protective shield around the Earth. As they watched, an invisible force seemed to meet this barrier in an explosion of coloured gaseous clouds flaring and fluxing with an equal intensity for about 25 seconds. Then it seemed to dissipate and move on as quickly as it had arrived.

"According to the long range scanners, the composition of those clouds, or whatever they were, would have destroyed every living creature, plant life everything in seconds had it not been protected by that force field."

The vidreport erupted in a cacophony of human noise, as the entire fleet burst onto the airwaves seeking clarification and standing orders before subsiding and levelling off as the immediate panic subsided and normality returned with the sounding of the "All Clear".

Rick nodded thoughtfully. "Well now that we………."

He stopped mid-sentence as a 10 foot high section of the wall in front of them became firstly translucent then resolved into a fixed image. Dhoran appeared from the left of the picture, dominating the scene in the transport chamber.

"Now it is time to talk!" His disembodied voice seemed to boom out at them as they heard the message from the image of a striking looking man whose lips didn't move. John half expected a time-delay in the image, but none came.

"Commander, have your troops enter the transport now arriving. It is time that we meet. You and Rick will join me here shortly."

Dhoran turned as if to leave, but John stilled him with a terse response.

"Just who are you and just where might "here" be mister! Nobody moves unless I say they do."

"All of you questions will be answered Commander. We must combine our forces now in alliance to eliminate one final threat to both your people, your world and mine. Please take your seats." If Dhoran had been taken by surprise he showed no sign of it, nor the suggestion of irritation; just the merest hint of amusement touched the corners of his mouth.

"Go ahead John, it's OK" assured Rick. "Believe me, he is one of the "good guys". Whatever he is going to tell us we will simultaneously broadcast to the fleet, the President, and the world population in general. I have a feeling that this part will really blow our minds!"

CHAPTER TWENTY-ONE: CELEBRATIONS

Jasmine and Mike just sat and stared at each other for what seemed like an eternity. The screen behind them had eventually cleared to show them Earth, still serene and safe in all her glory, hanging there against the black back-cloth beautifully blue, white and green. The remnants of the protective beam had all but cleared now that the danger had passed by. Dhoran sank back into his chair and locked fingers under his chin in contemplation. He allowed himself the luxury of the briefest of congratulations before switching his monitor to standby.

"We did it Jas!" was all that Mike could think of to say. Physically and emotionally drained they went through the routine of shutting down their Quorum team banks as if on autopilot.

"Jack are you OK?"

"Sure Mike, I'm fine, I think!"

Dhoran seized this moment to clasp each of their hands in turn, a gesture of sincere thanks to his friends.

"We have succeeded where none before has triumphed over Nature. Earth is safe forever more from this wretched cycle of needless destruction. But now we must turn our attentions to the enemy within. Look!"

Jack and Mike joined Dhoran at the console. The multi-split screen showed several menacing looking transports in motion.

"These are the cohorts of Paul Gregot intent on wresting this power from us on their way here to this Central Control. But we do have help now."

The view changed again, this time showing Earthforce Troopers riding open topped transports with their prisoners clearly and firmly restrained and under guard. Jasmine was standing a few metres away in font of a viewscreen showing the last of the transports arriving at the terminal. Mike moved towards her as she stood transfixed by the picture.

"How can this be Mike?" she said quietly as his arms enfolded her. "I saw him dead, I held his body in my arms, I...I... threw his bod......" She dissolved in tears against his chest, still half watching, half disbelieving the picture of Rick as if she expected it to fade away. All Mike could do was to hold onto her. He had no answers; he was no wiser than she as to what had happened here.

"Jasmine." Dhoran softened his voice as he came to her. "That is indeed your father. We felt it necessary to keep the real truth from you, for fear that you might be recaptured by Paul. Rick was vital in securing the base from the enemy and if Paul knew he had not killed him, the struggle might have been much worse."

"You knew this all along? Mike did you know?" Jasmine pleaded tearfully.

"No Jas, I'm as stunned as you are. Dhoran, why? This just seems so unnecessary?"

"Then let me explain it myself!" boomed the unmistakable voice of Rick. They all turned to witness the arrival of Earthforce with Rick heading up the column of victorious troopers. They all remained rooted to the spot apart from Jasmine who hurled herself at his imposing figure. "Dad! Dad! Thank God you are alive!" He held her gently until he felt her relax and release her grip on him, his own eyes uncharacteristically wet too.

"You had to be convinced it was for real for your own safety and to release you to act independently. Obviously it worked with spectacular results, I'm so proud of you! As to how it was, well we have Mike's father to thank for that too." He acknowledged Mike warily as if not sure what to expect. Seeing no outward sign of hostility he continued. "A top secret spin-off of the Quorum effect to be precise. Tom was working on it the night he died. The process allowed us to concentrate the usual multiple projections into a single entity which gave it the solidity of the original, even down to texture and mass. It made for a great decoy! We suspected Paul's treachery for some time, both Tom and I had our suspicions and we were determined to flush him out. He was a very smart operator, seemed to know in advance every move we made. We finally revealed him for what he really is Jas. He is not one of us, he is one of Dhoran's kind, but a bad one. This facility was deigned as multi-pupose. When Exodus took the people away from Earth, or Terrania as it was known to them, they decided to leave their criminal element behind in permanent sleep. They and the undesirables were put in Cryogenic stasis, in supposedly fail-safe conditions. Somehow Paul rigged a breakout. He arranged for his containment cell to be operated from inside, with a built in release timer. Immediately after the "Event" he escaped the facility and made straight for Earth where he had prepared his own bunker many years before. He managed to release an unknown number of his followers complete with drones along with him, of them there is still no trace other than his elite "guard" here. He then imposed his own form of exile on Earth, awakening at pre-set intervals to evaluate the conditions. Apparently the conditions as they exist today on our world suited his objectives perfectly. He knew of the work done here by Dhoran, his intention was to seize control of it all along, and with its power dominate and control our destiny in his own image. He did not have all the answers however. He did not know enough of the facility to prevent the next Event taking place. He had to get to Dhoran before we could find him to make sure his plan was fulfilled, and he almost succeeded. We were getting nowhere until you and Mike arrived together on the scene. The defence capability of this station is equally as powerful as a weapon in the wrong hands. Mankind would have been held to ransom in his unrelenting quest for power and domination. Incredible as it seems, this man was willing to sacrifice his lifetime several times over in pursuit of his own idea of an ideal. All that is left now is to find him and put him away permanently. With the help of the rearguard Earthforce troops docking at the outer ports of the facility, we should accomplish that goal too. Have I missed anything Dhoran?"

"Only the fact that as we are on the verge of concluding this most disagreeable debacle, I feel I should tell you in shame that Paul Gregot is in fact my son"

True enough, Dhoran's help was invaluable in tracking down and finally overcoming the desperate and suicidal tactics of Paul's elite guard before they were unceremoniously dumped and secured in the innermost and most heavily fortified cells of the complex. Here they were held in frozen state to await trial and punishment at the hand of none other than Dhoran himself who had been appointed Judge of Court for the trial of Paul Gregot as a traitor and danger to all mankind by grace of the Government of Earth in recognition of his contribution to the salvation of the Earth itself.

Watching from the far side of the hastily prepared Conference Chamber, the very one he had first encountered on entering the complex, Mike observed Jasmine as she talked quietly now with Rick When the two of them had been reunited he had felt a pang of both jealousy and a feeling of deja-vu as she had launched herself at him with the same fervour and energy of a tigress as she had done when he himself had rescued her. How long ago was that? He had listened patiently as she overcame the initial shock of Rick's survival and listened with increasing incredulity at the stories of the battle for the Moon against Paul's forces and the race to activate the defence mechanism. He himself had spent many days now it seemed in endless media interviews as news agencies from all over the World begged for their rights to his exclusive story. He hated every minute spent away from her now as he realised how much time they had wasted. Jack on the other hand seemed like a natural, relishing the spotlight and revelling in his new found fame. Mike was quick to appoint him as their official spokesperson. Even so as one of the most famous people on Earth now, he still had a fair proportion of important people to deal with. At the end of the day, when all the excitement had died down, he would still have a living to earn, so he resolved to use these new found contacts for future reference. Even so he resented every intrusion that meant them spending time apart. As he averted his gaze elsewhere, he noticed that it was not just he himself feeling the pressure of this media scramble. Dhoran was standing a little way off in deep discussion with a group of media people all vying for his attention at once. He looked decidedly irritated by the melee and kept himself well protected behind a posse of minders and military looking types. He had made a point on the cessation of fighting that Earthforce Command had total access to his entire facility. In truth whilst they had a fundamental knowledge of its operation, he was still the key to so much unknown application of technology, and they guarded him with fanatical thoroughness. That part rankled him even more than the Press, but at least he understood the reason behind the close cover. At first wary of the "alien", Earth Command had little option but to take him on trust. He had after all saved the Earth. This was warmly and deservedly recognised in the President's unashamed declaration of Dhoran as a Free Citizen of the World, an honour afforded to very few people at all.

Down on planet Earth, celebrations were still in full swing. As well as relief at their deliverance from an unseen and unsuspected menace, there was pervading sense of general euphoria and elation at the prospects of the dawning of a new era of progress and development. Many also felt it was like the beginning of a new adventure. Natural enough feelings given the prospects they had been facing only days earlier

Arrangements were well advanced for the repatriation of the remaining survivors of the Lunar One settlement. Of the original 3000 feared dead, after the disaster of the dome itself and the body count of the hapless victims of the underground firefight, all but 700 would be returning home to Earth. In their honour, the 700 would be honoured with an obelisk at the site of the former colony. They had been found safe and well, if a little disoriented, after an enforced short period of cryogenic sleep in one of the last of the cryogenic chambers to be revealed. At Dhorans direction, room after room of the eerily empty pods had been inspected. He explained that one part of his original plan had involved a fallback plan to save as many of the population in this way until Earth itself recovered and they could return to rebuild and repopulate. He confessed to being glad that it had not been necessary to take that particular option. Who would choose those to save and those to leave to their fate? Certainly not he. Thankfully in one way the Exodus option had avoided that particular problem totally. Eventually satisfied that they were all of the same status, the Security team had merely acknowledged the presence of the 1000 or more marked facilities on their schematics.

Dhoran had other responsibilities and titles bestowed upon him; some more reluctantly than others. He did accept the position of "Governor of the Moon" more easily than any of the others. He felt at home and at one with his creation and in truth knew more of its true nature and secrets than any other living being. So for all practical purposes, it gave his appointment credibility beyond the gesture intended. Now in the relaxed atmosphere after the Event, he was able to divulge more of its capabilities and features, not least its latent potential as a weapon of mass destruction. When they understood the magnitude of the threat this offered Earth, the Establishment almost freaked out yet again as they struggled to come to terms with the pace of the revelation of so much undiscovered technology around them.

At least one of the longest standing mysteries of the old "Moon" was revealed. During its construction, the interior of the satellite had been scooped out to accommodate the mass of electronics and control mechanisms needed for the device. Once complete the spoil was distributed over the surface in a crust of powdered rock. Early space exploration of the surface had often faced the vexed question of reverse dating of the upper levels of dust. The readings suggested that the surface layer was older than the layers below it. Now, the reason for that was finally clear.

CHAPTER TWENTY-TWO: FOREBODING

At last, Jasmine made her way across the throng of military and civilian personnel occupying the centre of the Conference Hall. Smiling up at him as she coyly entwined her fingers with his she looked wonderful in her hastily acquired civilian outfit, light-years away from the drab overalls she'd worn up until the official stand-down of martial law.

"Well now, Mr Hero, how are you feeling?" she asked in her usual irreverent manner reserved for their more private moments.

"Deprived, depressed and devastated," he replied, "but all is forgiven now that you're here with me!"

"Aw shucks honey, y'all gonna make me blush now!" she continued to mock him.

Yes they were most definitely back together, this time no force on Earth, or the Moon for that matter, was going to get in their way ever again. He smiled now as they held each other close gently swaying together.

"I'm so glad and relieved that you and Rick finally declared a truce." she said absently.

"I feel such an idiot about all of that," he replied as he nuzzled her hair. He inhaled its sweet freshly washed scent and buried his forehead in the glossy fullness. Rick had been anxious and careful to reveal the part he had played in the subterfuge following Tom's death. He knew shortly after it had happened about Paul's involvement in the murder, but had to hold this in check in order to reveal the true nature of his aide's betrayal. Paul Gregot was an impostor. With a superior level of intelligence, he had considered himself to be beyond suspicion. But Rick had picked up on one or two traits that didn't ring true and that he was not what he appeared to be. His behaviour during the excavation work and his ability to interpret complex alien controls and symbols was just too convenient to be true and inconsistent with his "declared" background of a non-technical type. Calling in a good many favours from some of his less well known associates, Rick had uncovered anomalies in Paul's background to reveal huge gaping chasms everywhere. Using the latest stealth technology and surveillance, every move Paul had made over a 5-year period had been carefully recorded and logged. On an unscheduled visit to Easter Island, the surveillance finally paid off. After trekking deep into the island's interior, Paul had opened and entered a deep subterranean complex similar in design to the complex they had discovered on the Moon. Rick's operative, a shadowy figure at best but a very effective one, had been able to follow and report back with pictures and drawings of much of the equipment and materials stored there. In fact the very same entry system they had encountered on the Moon was used at this complex. No wonder then that he had easily "broken" the entry code that first time. Without knowing it, Paul had himself helped Rick to plot his downfall. Amongst some of the data retrieved, they had come across mention of Dhoran's name along with some basic information about the lunar complex. The information had been of sufficient detail to lead Rick towards Dhoran's location and more importantly, his function in the Lunar complex itself. He had resolved to track Dhoran down and revive him from his self-induced exile and frozen sleep. He had been on the verge of making the contact itself when the events on the Lunar surface overtook him and his cover to Paul was blown.

However he managed to evade discovery long enough to contact and advise the most powerful of men in the President himself of the threat posed. With his full knowledge and assent and the help of several of the most elite scientists, they had hatched an elaborate plot to "discover" the Lunar complex's secret under the guise of a subversive "commercial" operation designed to flush Paul out into the open and destroy his ambition to total power and control.

Only now that he was safely locked away awaiting judgement of his treachery and violence did the truth emerge. Paul was the youngest of Dhoran's four sons. Against the directive of Exodus, and totally unknown to Dhoran himself, Paul had elected to stay and endure indefinite stasis on the pretext that if he could not continue to enjoy the world as he knew it, he preferred to sacrifice life itself. He had managed to get himself a place in the Lunar Colony's bank of cryogenic warehouses. Using his "contacts" and "associates" he had ensured that his particular rig was specially designated for him. It had of course been prepared with an early reawakening in mind. Outwardly the same as millions of others, the readings it gave out were false. One month after the event an automatic encoded sequence reactivated the pod and he emerged unchallenged. Once awake, he had taken the last remaining Launch Craft and returned to Earth to his carefully concealed survival complex on Easter Island. Once safely entombed and certain of non-detection, he had sealed off the entrance using the particle molecular synthesiser technology. In this way he had endured many millennia of enforced hibernation, emerging once in a while to assess the progress of the ensuing civilisations until he was satisfied that this one was worth exploiting. But for Rick's courage and tenacity and Mike's determination to see justice done for his father, Paul might have got his way. In Dhoran's mind, whatever the mitigating circumstances brought to the court in defence of his own son's actions, there could be only one verdict. Death!

"Hey Jas, let's go for a spin through the complex before we leave? Now that all of the passages are operational again, it might be our only chance of an uninterrupted tour ever again!" He then added in a quieter tone "And it might be the last chance to be alone with each other for a while too" he added with a smile.

Jasmine smiled back at him as she led him towards the transport bay. As they got to the platform she shook off his hand and scampered towards the waiting carriage. "Only if I can drive!" she squealed jumping into the two-man pod first. Mike made it just before the darkened shield closed over his head, and hurriedly strapped himself in as she engaged the drive. Kids once more, they exhilarated at the thrusting acceleration and giggled uncontrollably, partly from fear and partly with unbridled joy, as the carriage careered onwards spiralling in 360 degree turns around the tunnel walls in its headlong dash. Eventually they engaged the dampening fields and gravity pulse mode before shrugging off their harnesses followed almost immediately by their clothes.

"This will be a first!" said Jasmine.

"Yeah, something to tell the kids for sure!"

"Sooner than you think!" she smiled as she surrendered to his touch.

Dhoran left the VIP lounge, thankful at least that the President's address had diverted attention away from him at long last. Even though he resented the intrusiveness of the media circus, he did feel a certain pride and satisfacion that at last, though delayed by many thousands of years, his accomplishments had finally been recognised and appreciated. Perhaps another lifetime of work would be worthwhile after all, amongst this descendant race. The shame of the actions of his own offspring was a terrible burden for him to bear easily. Perhaps in some way his contribution to this generation could make up for some of that. He could scarcely believe that he could have spawned such a monster. Yet he could not feel altogether surprised at the outcome. Of all his children, Lloran, or Paul as he became, had always been the most wayward and most difficult in his upbringing. It had taken him several selections of guardians and tutors to get the boy through his first lifetime educated to Independence. From thereon, he had become a brilliant scholar and scientist, absorbing every scrap of knowledge with a voracity and appetite that seemed insatiable. This had pleased him after such a difficult start, the fact that perhaps after all he would have another son to be proud of. Sadly they had become distant with each other for many years until Dhoran's discovery brought Lloran back home. He had shown a keen desire to work with him on the project, absorbing every detail of his father's findings. Dhoran had long since realised that this new found "affection" was nothing more than Lloran's drive for power fuelled by greed and obsession with domination. That obsession had come very close to destroying all he had worked for and almost succeeded in delivering the power craved.

He took a monopod out and away from the Conference Hall. Entering the familiar codes, he sat back and relaxed for the duration of the journey to his Central Command Centre. At the terminus, he alighted and made for his quarters. He acknowledged the other transport as that of his newfound family Mike and Jasmine. They were waiting for him now at the end of the platform.

"Dhoran! Thank goodness it's you! There are some weird transmissions coming in, we can't decipher them.

And that's not all. Your display panel has come to life for some reason, we didn't activate it. We sure hope you know what's going on 'cause we sure as Hell don't!"

Dhoran sensed the reason behind their frivolous playacting, but he forgave them instantly. After all, they were not to know the significance of the insistent signal chiming out audibly now from the speaker. He double-checked for any malfunction first before backing away from the panel shaking his head in disbelief.

"Dhoran, what is it?" Jasmine was the first to recover her senses as she saw the visible change in Dhoran's attitude. There was genuine concern in her voice.

"They….. they….. they have returned!" he gasped as he sank to his knees with his head in his hands in anguish.

Before they could quiz him further, the signal for General Alert sounded out. The pattern was a Red Alert. Mike quickly linked up the centre with communications.

"Commander, this is Mike Brett at Central Command Centre. What's the problem, what's going on?"

"Mike, turn on your external sensors. We're picking up multiple images of what appear to be attack ships ---------- and they're not ours!"

As Mike flicked over to the external sensors, the screen resolved into static before jumping to a transmission configuration he'd never seen before. Dhoran made an adjustment with a shaking hand. The screen cleared to reveal a black visored figure in a black uniform heavily adorned with braid and insignia. For their benefit he engaged the translator.

"We are the Outcasts of Terrania! We come to reclaim our birthright. Any resistance will be met with total force. Do not oppose us! We are many million strong! Surrender now or meet your fate in War!"

"Petranhan! Terranian Prime Commander!" Dhoran spoke in whispers. "They have returned after all this time! But they have a New World, how can this be?"

He turned to face Mike and Jasmine.

"This is not good. These are the people of Earth from my time. They left to colonise the new planet we discovered. Now they have returned to reclaim their ancient Terrania. What will you do?"

Jasmine and Mike looked at one another and spoke as one.
"We fight!"

Deep within the complex, long dormant lighting panels broke the eternal darkness below them. As if in answer to the intrusion of light into their silent and dark space, 100,000 cryochambers simultaneously lit up, their readouts in synchronised countdown. 1000 concealed and buried ships waited patiently for the return of their long dormant crews.

In the loneliness of his frozen world of sleep, Paul mentally smiled as the deadline approached and he waited in anticipation of his next release.

ABOUT THE AUTHOR

From a childhood featuring the likes of Dan Dare and Flash Gordon to the present with Darth Vader and Skywalker, George has been an avid sci-fi aficionado.

After years of absorbing the best of such inspirational masters like Asimov and Arthur C. Clarke, he has evolved his own opinions and attitudes about the portrayal of the more flamboyant and exotic futures in current circulation, offering a more pragmatic "down to earth" realism in his writing.

Throughout his novel, he captures the potential realities of our evolution, interlacing technical advances with undertones of the commercial motivators of corporate and individual greed, reflecting some of his own commercial real-life experiences through the characters.

Printed in the United Kingdom
by Lightning Source UK Ltd.
107471UKS00001B/12